A Father Before Christmas

A Father Before Christmas

NEIL BOYD

BOOK CLUB ASSOCIATES LONDON

Printed in Great Britain by
Richard Clay (The Chaucer Press), Ltd.,
Bungay Suffolk

For
M and F and D
With Love

CONTENTS

A FATHER BEFORE CHRISTMAS

One

MY FIRST BAPTISM

'That uproarious wretch, that blighted black-eyed potato of a woman.' Fr Charles Duddleswell, my parish priest, was performing on the landing.

'What's up?' I said, poking my head round my study door.

'Me keys,' he snapped, his blue eyes frothing behind his steel-rimmed spectacles. 'Can I find me keys? Indeed I cannot. Mrs Pring has filched them from me dresser and neither she nor the blessèd St Anthony has any idea where she has deposited them.'

I took one look at him and said, 'You've tried your pockets, Father?'

'Is it an idiot you think I ...?' He was busy scratching the smooth outer skin of his cassock like an itchy monkey. 'In me pockets?' he asked now only half in scorn. 'Me pockets, you say?' His hand had settled around a bulky something in his bottom left pocket. He slowly brought the keys into the light of day. 'That accursèd daughter of Eve,' he muttered, 'has she not hidden 'em in the recesses of me very own pocket?' He suddenly yelled down the staircase. 'Mrs Pring!'

Unhurriedly our plump, white-haired Mrs Pring appeared at the foot of the stairs, clasping a broom like a crosier. 'You've found them, then,' she said, 'I'll get the choir to sing the *Te Deum* in thanksgiving.'

' 'Twas not meself that found them,' came thundering back at her, 'but Father Neil.'

'And *where* did he find them?'

'Does it at all matter, woman, where he found them, seeing as he found them?'

Mrs Pring suggested none too politely that they had never gone missing.

'Woman,' he cried, 'I will not have you coming at me with a full udder of incivility. Now, I am asking you, could Father Neil have found them if they were never lost? Father Neil,' he bellowed in my direction, 'would you be so kind as to inform this lady, who is astray of her wits, that you ...'

But I retreated into my study to let them sort out for themselves who was to blame for losing Fr Duddleswell's enormous bunch of keys in his cassock pocket.

I settled down again and opened my breviary but I was in no mood for praying. I preferred that October morning to reflect on my career thus far at St Jude's.

Four crowded months had passed since I first presented myself at the presbytery door, to be greeted by Mrs Pring and the uncertain sound of *Gilbert and Sullivan* coming from Fr Duddleswell's hand-cranked gramophone. I was at that time, I recalled with a smile, as green and helpless as a pea from the pod.

By now, I was used to hearing confessions and no longer feared I would forget the formula of absolution in the middle. Preaching, while not a pleasure, had ceased to be a torment. I enjoyed taking Holy Communion to the elderly and the bed-ridden and they were always genuinely pleased to see me.

It wasn't so bad visiting people in their homes once I was inside. There was always a moment just before I knocked or rang when the devil put it into my heart to wonder whether I should call again some other day. I was particularly daunted by three old tenement buildings, known locally as Stonehenge, in the middle of my patch. They had no lights and no lifts. Most of the stone steps were chipped or broken and they smelled of carbolic or worse. Often there were no numbers on the doors. I had to take pot luck, whisper 'Come Holy Ghost', and hope to God I had come to the right place. It never mattered. Non-Catholics were invariably polite to 'the cloth' and keen to redirect me to where lapsed Catholics were hiding out. Sometimes I was sure they were zealous in helping me find my lost sheep out of spite, and I admit I was relieved whenever I received no answer. The Lord could not accuse me of not trying even if the results of my labours were negative.

Continuing the habit of years I exchanged letters with my mother every couple of weeks. The family were well. My salary was only £40 a year—Fr Duddleswell paid me for the first quarter in half-crowns—but this was supplemented by Mass stipends which, at five shillings a time and sometimes more, brought in another £2 a week. There were other sources of income too. At St Jude's there had recently been several weddings, a funeral and a dozen baptisms. Fr Duddleswell had officiated at all of them but he had shared out the proceeds, called stole-fees. He did not mention how he divided them but my portion was so generous I never doubted that he gave me half. Board and lodging were free so I was able for the first time in my life to send the occasional postal order to my younger brothers and sisters who were still at school. I missed them, especially on Bank Holidays when there was nothing for me to do and nowhere to go.

There were other gains besides my new-found affluence. I had my very own radio. Though it was an old three valve model and crackled as if it were permanently on short-wave, it did enable me to listen to the news and find out what was happening in the world. In the seminary, I was not allowed a newspaper or magazine, except *The Catholic Herald*. I had read only half a dozen novels in my life. Their contents were far too trivial and worldly for one with his sights on eternal things.

My greatest gain at St Jude's was living alongside Fr Duddleswell and Mrs Pring. My parish priest, who claimed to be 'as old and whiskered as a bog mist', had taught me the value of discretion. 'Open wide your heart, Father Neil,' was his advice, 'but fasten down the shutters of your mind. Should you turn your head inside-out in front of the good people where is the use? 'Twill only worry and confuse them and have they not enough complications in their lives already, like?' As for Mrs Pring, she was a staunch ally who showed in a hundred quiet ways that she cared for me. Their altercations seldom involved me, and the intensity of them, I sensed, was an index of their mutual regard.

I was even developing a fondness for urban life. After years of being surrounded by rolling hills, trees, tractors and grazing cows, the town, particularly our district of Fairwater, had not initially appealed to me. It was by comparison noisy, dusty and congested. Greys predominated instead of greens. The wide sweep of the sky was foreshortened and broken up by T.V. aerials and chimney pots. But I was now able to find my way around. I knew the names of the streets and was beginning to recognize some of the faces of those who walked them. In spite of the coolness creeping into the October air, and the premature yellowing of the leaves on the city trees, I was content.

Ahead of me stretched the calmest months of the Church's year. No Lenten fast. No long Holy Week services. Only Advent as we prepared for the Coming of the Lord. Then

Christmas itself, the season of peace and goodwill.

There was a rap on my door.

'May the divil tear you from the hearse in front of all the funeral.' Fr Duddleswell was not addressing me; he was concluding his conversation with Mrs Pring over the disappearance of his keys.

Flushed with what he took for victory, he laughed: 'I have had quite enough of *her* babblement. That female would quarrel with her own two shins.'

He settled down to tell me how pleased he was to see me 'coming out like a flower', and to broaden the scope of my apostolate, he had arranged a christening for me on the following Sunday.

'Jimmy and Jeannie Dobbs are the parents, Father Neil. Good practising Catholics. Ditto the godparents. Nothing could be easier. And by the by, Father Neil, one important consideration.'

'Yes, Father?'

'Do not be so foolish as to leave your keys unchaperoned in this house. There is a lady tolerated here who has a propensity to conceal 'em in places no reasonable creature would pretend to look.' His eye had a lost, far-away look. 'Have I not just purchased her another vacuum cleaner, and she plays a trick on me like that?' He shook his head in secret despair. 'Ah, but it conflaberates me marvellously to see her standing idly by, swallowing herself with a yawn.'

Soon after he had gone, conflaberated, I could hear him exclaiming, 'Will you stop acting the maggot, woman, and start fisting that broom around yon filthy floor.' And Mrs Pring's stout reply: 'I'll put your request on the long finger, Fr D.'

I took my commission as a sign of Fr Duddleswell's growing confidence in me. I opened up my Roman Ritual to remind myself of my duties.

'Nothing could be easier,' he had said, and on the face of it he was right. But my experience of christening was limited to pouring water over the head of a doll under the somnolent eye of the Professor of Moral Theology in my last year at the seminary.

Canon Flynn had taught us that baptism is not valid if anything is used but water for washing. I remembered his emphasis on that phrase. 'Not liquids made up of water,' he said, 'which people do not normally use for washing. Not tea, therefore, nor coffee, neither beer nor lemonade.'

I took it for granted that Fr Duddleswell did not allow such beverages in his font.

As Sunday afternoon approached, my chief concern was to pronounce the baptismal formula while actually pouring water over the head. Simultaneity of words and action was essential for validity. I kept wishing I'd had more time to practise on that doll.

One thing I was determined to do was to read the formula from the book. According to Canon Flynn, it was only too easy after a while to repeat in Latin the confessional form, *I absolve you* instead of the baptismal form, *I baptize you.*

After Sunday lunch, Fr Duddleswell said, 'Make sure you put all the details in the book; names of the child, parents and godparents. And enter them legibly, Father Neil, not like Dr Daley writing out a prescription for mumps.'

These seemed matters of small consequence in the light of other disasters I could think of.

In the event, the christening was a relaxed family affair. Paul John Dobbs, three weeks old, was blue-eyed and as bald as a new lamb of the Flock should be. I read the vital words 'I baptize you in the name of the Father and of the Son and of the Holy Ghost' while pouring over him a liquid no Devil's Advocate would dare suggest was anything but Adam's ale. The baby did not cry at any stage of the ceremony, not even when I put the salt of wisdom on his tongue or poured autumnal water on his shiny head.

Afterwards, I filled in the baptism register, legibly, in capitals. As I closed the book, Mr Pickles, the godfather, coughed nervously and greased my palm with a pound note. I congratulated myself on the fact that everything had passed off better than I could have wished. And it was with a light heart that I accepted an invitation to the christening party at 1 Pimms Road, close by the railway junction.

The reception was as uncomplicated as the baptism itself. There was tea, cucumber sandwiches and trifle. The new Christian was lying asleep in his cradle next to the settee. When after half an hour he awoke, Mrs Dobbs, a sturdy north country girl and former teacher, picked him up. She dipped her fingers in a square shaped jar and started rubbing his head.

That was when my worries began.

I edged my way over to where Mrs Dobbs was sitting. 'What are you doing?' I asked as casually as I could.

'Rubbing his scalp, Father. A trick my mother taught me.'

'What with?'

'Vaseline. My mother swears it strengthens the roots.'

I did not want to know what Vaseline was supposed to do because of my fear at what it had already done. Vaseline was waterproof. What if the baptismal water had not touched the baby's head at all? Trembling, I said, 'Do you do that often, Mrs Dobbs?'

'Three times a day at least, Father.'

'This morning, too?'

She nodded, tickled by my interest in the number of times

17

she rubbed her child's head with Vaseline, I swigged my tea, blindly shook a circle of hands, and said goodbye.

'Please come again soon, won't you, Father,' said Mrs Dobbs. It was an invitation for which I had reason subsequently to be grateful.

I walked the sound proof Sunday afternoon streets wrestling with the overwhelming problem posed by that Vaseline. I was beginning to understand how Canon Flynn's national reputation as a moralist had been won. He had warned us repeatedly that many mothers saturate their babies' heads with creams, oils, lotions.

'Take care,' he had said, 'that the water flows over the child's scalp. Not merely the hair. Hair is composed of dead cells and is only doubtfully identifiable with the living child. See to it that there's no protective coating of cream on his head otherwise'—one of his rare jokes—'it might protect him from becoming a Christian.'

The sacrament of baptism, I reflected, is a sign of washing. Unless the water *flows* and *washes* the body, there is no sacramental sign and thus no cleansing of the soul. God has a right, I have to admit, to lay down certain requirements for salvation. His demands are not harsh but his ministers, especially after six years of preparation, have their part to play. What if I have sent away a pagan instead of a Christian from the font?

Madly, I switched from self-pity to self-loathing and back. My mother used to say that when a baby cries at a christening it is only the devil going out of him. An old wives' tale. Still, how I wished Paul had screamed blue murder at the font.

Surely God was not so arbitrary or cruel as to deprive a child of the grace of baptism simply because a fond mother had spread a film of Vaseline on his head? Yet I had heard of a child being killed on a level-crossing while his mother was pushing him to church to be christened. No Catholic theologian, as far as I knew, had ever suggested that the poor little mite could get to Heaven. The consensus was that the child was borne to Limbo care of British Railways. Why, then, had the Church discarded the earliest and by far the safest method of baptism—by immersion?

'Mighty pleased I am to see you taking the air, Father Neil.'

It was Fr Duddleswell on a late afternoon stroll after his siesta. He was sporting the kind of floppy, broad-brimmed hat that artists wear. Would he be able to read the guilt written in capitals on my face?

'Hope I did not interrupt your meditation, like?'

I shook my head and agreed to walk with him to the Embankment. Soon, with our backs to the line of trees, we were leaning on the black wall overlooking the rust-coloured waters of the Thames. Beyond, on the south side, were wharves and cranes and tall chimneys spewing out grey smoke. I brought the conversation round to baptism by handing over the stole-fee for the christening. To accept any part of it would have been to add crookedness to incompetence.

'How did it go this afternoon, Father Neil?' Before I could answer, he said, 'And tell me, now, did you write all the details clearly in the register?'

I assured him of that. It set his mind at rest. How trivial the concerns and quiet the soul of the seasoned campaigner.

'Funny thing, Father,' I began.

'What is that?'

'Baptism. Making a Christian with a few words and less than half a pint of water.'

19

'*Unless a man be born again of water and the Holy Ghost,*'
he replied, quoting Jesus' words to Nicodemus. 'John's
Gospel, Chapter three, verse five. Our Blessed Lord's
disciples must all have been baptized, saving His Holy
Mother naturally who was conceived without original sin.'

I put it to him that other Christians are not as careful as
Catholics in administering the sacrament.

'The eastern Orthodox are,' he insisted. 'But I agree with
you, not the Protestants. To start with, I do not think three
quarters of them believe in original sin. And—you will not
credit this, mind—it has come to me ears that our Anglican
friend the Rev. Percival Probble sometimes baptizes several
babies at once. Sprinkles them. Not so much as a cat's lick.
Well, you know how 'tis at the Asperges before High Mass.
Not everyone is so fortunate as to get splashed in the eye with
Holy Water. No matter. They are Christians already. Deprived of a few hundred days Indulgence they may be, but
they can compensate for that by bowing their head at the
Holy Name. But baptism, now, that is another kettle of fish
altogether.' His eyes swept over the Thames as though it
were the Styx. 'God alone knows how many innocent babes
who die in infancy are deprived of the Beatific Vision because of the negligence of foreign clergymen.'

I was not deriving any comfort from the conversation.
'The river's high today,' I said.

Undeterred, he continued, 'If the water does not reach the
body, where is the sacrament, Father Neil?'

I was too wounded to reply.

'D'you know,' he went on, 'I had not long ago a most un-
typical case.' He paused to let a noisy barge go by. 'There
was this Spanish lass of seventeen summers came to me to get
married. I told her: "Write your parish priest in Barcelona
for your baptism and confirmation certificates me darlin."

He sent back word of her confirmation but said all baptismal registers had been burned in the Civil War. I spoke to Bishop O'Reilly about her and he said, "You will have to baptize her again conditionally to be on the safe side, like." Well, God save us, Father Neil, I confides to meself, has not our microdot of a Bishop this time surpassed himself in caution. After all, the Señorita had received Holy Communion every Sunday for a score of years, had she not? But what d'you suppose, Father Neil?' I tried without success to keep my mind a blank. 'Her mother owned up. Her daughter had been born just prior to the Red occupation. She was too terried to have her baptized before and too negligent after.'

'Baptism of desire,' I suggested, clutching at a theological wisp too thin to be called a straw.

He agreed. 'But think of the many graces and blessings she has been deprived of all her life. And what is more, her Confirmation and all the Holy Communions were *invalid* because she was not even a baptized Christian.'

Once more I tried to change the subject but failed.

'Give credit to the Bishop, Father Neil. Had we sailed ahead with the wedding without baptizing the Señorita, 'twould not have counted in the sight of God. Never would she have become a Señora and ...'

I could see him visualizing a great brood of illegitimate Spanish babies filing by under the sad gaze of God the Almighty.

In the days that followed, my mind was preoccupied with the spiritual state of Paul John Dobbs. Why are souls invisible so you can't see what is going on in them? If I *had* failed in my first Christening and if, God forbid, Paul died before the age of reason, he would be consigned to Limbo together with that unfortunate baby who was mowed down by a train.

Limbo, the Church teaches, is a place of perfect natural felicity. But it's not the same as Heaven where Paul's Catholic parents had every right to expect to find him when they eventually arrived. It was no consolation to me to know that my mistake would only be detected 'on the other side'.

The nights were terrible. I could not sleep. At manic speed, I went over a song from *Iolanthe* which, until then, I'd not been aware I knew by heart.

> *When you're lying awake with a dismal headache*
> *And repose is tabooed by anxiety*
> *I conceive you may use any language you choose*
> *To indulge in without impropriety*
> *For your brain is on fire, the bedclothes conspire*
> *Of usual slumber to plunder you*
> *First your counterpane goes and uncovers your toes*
> *And your sheet slips demurely from under you ...*

All the verses. In four seconds flat. At the same time, I kept telling myself that Paul was a perfectly healthy little boy. He was sure to survive to the age of seven and qualify for the baptism of desire. No Limbo for him, only the straight choice set before every grown up soul of Heaven or Hell. On the debit side, I conceded he would be deprived of the Church's sacraments like Fr Duddleswell's Señorita. And there would be no intervention of the Bishop in his case to stop him becoming an unmarried husband and father.

Then came a night which I classified unhesitatingly as the worst of my life.

About one o'clock I took three sleeping tablets and drifted into a restless sleep. In my dream I saw Paul, handsome and upright in his late teens. Not being a Señorita, he was able to enter a seminary. He was ordained a priest. It was invalid, of course. Due to my negligence he was still a pagan. I pictured him offering daily Mass, dispensing Communion, giving hundreds of absolutions—all of them invalid, too. I saw him anointing the dying. Many of these poor creatures, thinking quite reasonably that Paul was a genuine priest, had not sufficient contrition to merit final forgiveness of their sins. They ended up, surprised and aggrieved, in the wrong place where they cursed me heatedly for ever and ever.

The irony was that the only sacrament Paul was able to administer validly was the one which a film of Vaseline had deprived him of: baptism. Even laymen can baptize if they take proper care.

The depths were about to be plumbed. Paul, having been ordained, was consecrated bishop. Looking for all the world like Bishop O'Reilly, he handed on Holy Orders tirelessly, but his ordinations, unbeknown to anyone but God, did not 'take'. I saw in consequence hundreds of supposed priests dispensing hundreds of supposed sacraments year after year, century after century. In the diocese where Paul reigned there was a kind of huge, spiritual emptiness. No grace, no sacraments, no Christian hope. In that benighted place, the Catholic Church was no better off than the Church of England whose orders Leo XIII had solemnly declared in 1896 to be invalid.

I awoke in a sweat and with a fiercely pumping head, grateful that Paul had not gone on to become Pope. It was three o'clock. Certain that I would not sleep again that night, I stepped into my slippers and crept downstairs to the kitchen to make myself a cup of tea. While I was waiting for the kettle to boil I thought I heard a click. In normal circumstances I would have had no difficulty in identifying it but there was so much clamour inside my head I was not bothering about a tiny noise outside.

I was sitting at table about to sip my tea when I heard a car racing in the direction of the presbytery. It screeched to a halt near the front door. From the hall came the sound of the bolts being hastily drawn and Fr Duddleswell's conspiratorial voice, 'In there.' Fast, heavy footfalls in the street, then in the hall. Next, the whole kitchen seemed suddenly to contract as it filled with uniformed men breathing heavily and mouthing obscenities to keep their spirits up.

As I sprang up my right arm was gripped in a vice and pinioned behind my back. My head jerked back in a reflex action and thwacked my assailant somewhere about the face. He cried out in agony and released me. My relief was short-lived. Someone in front of me put the knee in, and I passed out.

I came round possibly a few seconds later in Mrs Pring's upholstered rocking chair. My eyes were watering, I felt sick and I had difficulty in breathing.

Fr Duddleswell was pouring a cup of cold water over my bowed head and slapping my cheek. I was dimly aware that Mrs Pring, cold-creamed, curlered, and in her dressing gown, had joined a misty throng. She was assuring Fr Duddleswell that 'poor Father Neil has been baptized already without you drenching him in my kitchen'. She took over from him and placed smelling salts under my nose of such potency my head was all but lifted from my shoulders.

Gradually the haze began to clear. I made out two policemen. One was applying a cold compress to his colleague's eye. It was puffy and purple. I would have shown sympathy had I not been preoccupied with nausea, and shooting pains in my infernal regions.

I heard Fr Duddleswell rambling on about new Hoovers and neighbourhood thieves who did wicked things with them, and Mrs Pring's obdurate tendency to mislay keys and to bolt the back door with a boiled carrot.

Mrs Pring soon set the room to rights and responded to Fr Duddleswell's request to 'wet the tay' for all. She offered me three steaming cups in her three right hands. 'You'll feel all the better, Father Neil, for pouring that down the red lane.'

P.C. Winkworth, who had nearly bisected me, slowly undid the button of his tunic and took out a notebook. As he came into focus, I saw his cap was off. His straw hair stood on end, topping a brown furrowed face and a small red nose. His head looked like a pineapple with a cherry stuck on. Nodding towards Mrs Pring, he said to Fr Duddleswell, 'Your Missis I take it, sir.'

Fr Duddleswell swelled indignantly as he drew in his breath. 'No, Constable, we only live together.' He made haste to explain that Mrs Pring was his housekeeper and that while she had a good pair of shoulders underneath her head they did not so much as share an opinion or a tube of toothpaste.

'I see, sir. And your name, please, sir.'

'Duddleswell. *Father* Duddleswell.'

'Is that prefix some sort of title, sir?'

My parish priest explained carefully his central role in the community.

'And this young man, I take it, sir,' the policeman said, indicating me, 'is an associate of yours?'

'I have not me spectacles on me nose, Officer, but his features bear an uncanny resemblance to me curate.'

'Am I to assume, sir,' the policeman plodded on, 'that you are not wanting to prefer charges?'

Fr Duddleswell looked at me sitting hunched up at the table clad in slippers and pyjamas. He was obviously at a loss to know what he could charge me with except the misfortune of being his assistant. 'No,' he said generously. 'If Father Neil is prepared to forget the incident, so am I.'

'Well,' went on P.C. Winkworth, 'that makes it rather difficult for us, sir. You see, sir, Central Control logged your call. They ordered us to proceed here. They will also be able to ascertain from the state of P.C. Richards's eye that the young gentleman over there assaulted a police officer while resisting arrest.'

It took my accuser ten minutes to accept that he had no legitimate cause to arrest a curate for sipping tea in his own kitchen even if he was responding to the invitation of the parish priest.

Eventually the two coppers left. Mrs Pring thereupon started badgering Fr Duddleswell for not letting the curate make himself a cup of tea at night without dialling 999 and summoning the police. 'Be careful, woman,' he threatened, 'for you are busy planting me with a mustard seed of wrath.'

I slunk upstairs throbbing in more places than one. I was still miserable and yet, for no reason I could pin down, I found myself repeating the lines, *But the darkness has past, And it's daylight at last.* As soon as my head hit the pillow, I fell into a dreamless sleep.

I awoke next morning at the usual time with a clear head and buoyant spirits, troubled only by a bruise below. I set about marshalling the facts.

It was not for me to turn my cranium inside out in front of the faithful. I could not go along to Mr and Mrs Dobbs and apologize for failing to baptize their infant. They had seen me do it. I could hardly expect them to appreciate the finer points of theology. Nor could I offer to rebaptize their son. That would be worse than a doctor re-inoculating a child because he had forgotten to put vaccine in the syringe the first time.

Poor Father Neil has been baptized already without you drenching him in my kitchen. Mrs Pring's words echoed in my mind. If *I* could be 're-baptized' in domestic surroundings, why not Paul John Dobbs? Fr Duddleswell had not scrupled to do that in the case of a little girl in Birmingham with far less justification than I now had. There was one important difference, of course. My baptism would be so private that even the parents themselves wouldn't know.

At breakfast, Fr Duddleswell tried to make light of 'last evening's entertainment'.

Mrs Pring brought him to a sharp halt with a special glower and went out.

'She will put a fat lip on her for a month of Sundays,' he complained. 'What can you expect of the unfair sex, Father Neil?' I smiled compliantly. 'Always remember when arguing with a woman that conclusive evidence does not prove a thing.' I promised to store away that pearl of wisdom. 'I was but doing me duty as I saw it, like. No hard feelings?'

'No,' I said, relieved that my problem was in principle resolved.

He squeezed my arm in gratitude. 'May you live as long as a proverb, Father Neil.'

On Thursday I went to Mrs Pring's kitchen for a morning cup of tea and to find out how long it takes a kettle of water to boil. I also picked a five inch shrimp paste jar with a screw-on lid out of the dustbin.

As soon as Fr Duddleswell left for the day, I crept into his study and borrowed the keys to the baptistery.

In church there was an annoying stream of parishioners praying before the Blessed Sacrament. It was nearly an hour before I could unlock the baptistery gates and the padlock on the font without being seen. Begging the Lord's pardon, I filled my jar with oily water from the font. After lunch, I remained in my study until 2.30 praying that Mr Dobbs would be at work and Paul conveniently placed for christening.

'Please come in, Father,' said Mrs Dobbs. 'Surprised to see you so soon.'

I was not sure whether this was a welcome or a rebuke for returning before my shadow was dry on the wall.

Paul was sleeping soundly in his cradle but to my dismay there was a neighbour present. Mrs Ivy Burns, a surly looking creature, had not been invited to the christening. Her hair was tied up in a kerchief so it looked as if she was carrying a workman's lunch on her head. I got the impression she could jabber on all day.

To justify my visit I had bought Paul a christening gift. I handed Mrs Dobbs a paper bag with 'Woolworth' in red on the outside.

Mrs Dobbs opened it up and took out a fire-engine. 'Oh, you shouldn't have, Father.'

'Bit young for it, ain't he?' croaked Mrs Burns, who was puffing away at her hand-rolled cigarette.

'It's for when he grows up,' I said.

'Like a cup of tea, Father?' asked Mrs Dobbs kindly.

With Mrs Burns there, my plan had misfired and I was out of pocket for nothing. 'No thank you. I've just had two large cups of coffee.'

I am not by nature impolite but it occurred to me there was a way to get rid of the intruder. I must keep my mouth shut. Whenever I was addressed by either of the ladies I replied with a nod or a shake of the head while looking Ivy stolidly in the eyes. Something had to give. Mrs Burns surrendered and took her leave. I immediately came to life, wished her a very warm goodbye and expressed the hope that our paths would cross again soon. Then I turned my attention to Paul's mother.

'Maybe I would, Mrs Dobbs.'

'*Would*, Father?'

'I would like a cup of tea, after all.'

'Good,' she said. If she was puzzled by my strange behaviour and sudden thirst she did not show it. 'I'll join you. I'll put the kettle on.'

I reckoned on having at least a minute while she was in the kitchen. As I stepped across to Paul's cradle I could hear Mrs Dobbs drawing water into the kettle. I had unscrewed the shrimp paste jar when Mrs Dobbs returned. I barely had time to thrust the jar into my left trouser pocket.

Mrs Dobbs, seeing me hovering and now cooing over her sleeping infant, came and stood beside me. In a whisper, she said, 'Our pride and joy, Father.'

'And rightly so,' I returned, as I felt cold water streaming down my leg.

'We've been married a year now.'

'Is he your first then?' I asked, not immediately taking in what she had said and shaking my leg uneasily.

I bent down slightly over Paul's reclining figure and from there could see my black herring-bone trousers turning all glossy at the crotch and down one leg. I hoped my woollen sock would soak up the water. I didn't want Mrs Dobbs to have to tell her husband that the curate, besides insulting Ivy Burns, had relieved himself on the dining room floor.

We stood there side by side gazing at Paul with widely differing emotions until a whistle from the kitchen signalled that the kettle was boiling.

'I'll make the tea, Father. Won't be long.'

'Take as long as you like, Mrs Dobbs.'

'Any biscuits?'

'Yes, lots, please.'

'I'll bring the tin so you can help yourself.'

My second and last chance. I took out the jar and was delighted to find it was still half full. Bending down, I whiffed the faint baby smell of ammonia. I rubbed a big patch of Paul's scalp with my handkerchief, then with unsteady hand poured what was left in the shrimp paste jar over it.

'*Paule, ego te baptizo ...*' I managed to finish the formula but not before the new Christian gave irrefutable evidence that the devil had gone out of him. Never have I seen so much trouble on such a tiny face. So stupendous was the caterwauling he emitted that his mother, though weighed down with a large tea tray, came running in.

Caught in that downward position I had no choice. I barely had a moment to wipe Paul's forehead, tuck the shrimp paste jar under the quilt and take him in my arms. 'I'm sorry, Mrs Dobbs,' I said, 'I must have disturbed him, so I picked him up.'

Seeing my evident fondness for her pride and joy, she relaxed and gave a smile of approval. 'I'll put this tray down, Father, then I'll take him. He may be a bit wet and I don't want him to christen *you*.' She blushed and apologized for her 'slip of the tongue'.

I handed Paul, still bawling, to his mother. He was transformed instantly into a whimpering bundle in her arms.

In essence, my mission was accomplished, but two problems remained. First, though the water spilt on Paul's bedding could be explained, I felt I ought to remove the shrimp paste jar. Only I or Ivy Burns could have put it there, and I couldn't see her taking the rap for me.

Second, I was sure that sooner or later Mrs Dobbs was bound to notice the wet patch on my trousers, far too large for a month-old baby in water-proof pants to have made.

I would solve both problems at once. 'Since you're holding the baby,' I said, 'why not let me pour?'

'That's very kind of you, Father.'

I filled a cup, made to pass it to her, and accidentally split the contents on my vitals. 'O my God!' I screamed, clutching myself immodestly in the spot where I was already wounded. Why hadn't I at least had the sense to put the milk in first?

My outburst roused Paul to fresh operatic heights. Mrs Dobbs, encircling him with one arm, proposed to fetch me a cloth from the kitchen.

In those precious seconds, through tears of pain, I retrieved the jar and returned it to my pocket.

Mrs Dobbs handed me a tea towel. I dabbed myself gently until the worst of the throbbing was over.

'Can I help in any way, Father?'

I said I didn't see how she could. She said she'd meant by calling a doctor or something.

'It's nothing, Mrs Dobbs, really. I'm maladroit, always doing careless things like this. I'm sure there won't even be a blister to speak of.'

After we had mopped up, we sat down and quietly drank our tea.

'Biscuit, Father?'

There was no need to explain my reluctance to prolong the visit, but before I left I gave Paul my blessing and a light-hearted pat on his head for luck.

Ah, I murmured when I was in the street, who would have thought it was such a costly business turning pagans into Christians?

Two

FEMME FATALE

I am no expert when it comes to jewelry but I couldn't help feeling that the rosary which the lady asked me to bless after Mass was strung with pearls. She thanked me in a quiet voice and handed me an envelope before threading her way through the emerging Sunday congregation. I watched her walk to a white Rolls Royce. As the chauffeur opened the door for her I spied two white, well groomed French poodles on the rear seat, yapping excitedly.

I returned to my study before opening the envelope. It was pink, embossed and scented. Inside was a £10 note.

Not knowing whether the reward for blessing a rosary was classed in the trade as a stole-fee, I put the matter to Fr Duddleswell. His immediate response was to rub his hands and say, 'Miss Davenport is back.'

Miss Davenport was the only child of a financier long dead. She had inherited everything, and *everything*, it appeared, was not a bad description of what she had inherited. The family business had continued to flourish because she took no interest in it. She was in the habit of passing each winter in a secluded Georgian house just over the border in the neighbouring parish of All Saints. If past experience was anything to go by, her patronage of St Jude's was likely to be generous.

'We will have less difficulty paying the schools' bills these next twelve month,' Fr Duddleswell forecast, 'provided we play our cards right. And for our part we can help this lady, too. Miss Davenport is, shall we say, a trifle whimsical? Promise me solemnly, now, that you will humour her.'

Not knowing then the full nature of her eccentricities but liking the first of them I'd met with, I gave him the assurance he sought. As to the money in the envelope, he said, enigmatically, that all things considered I was entitled to it this time.

That meeting on the church steps with Miss Davenport was the first of many. In the next two weeks she appeared daily at Mass—always at my Mass, whether I was celebrating the 7.30 or the 8 o'clock. Afterwards, she came into the sacristy as I was unvesting to ask me to bless a medal or a picture of the Sacred Heart. Each time she handed me a pink scented envelope. Thoroughly embarrassed by now, I told her that the parish was very grateful for her support and I would place her offering in the Poor Box.

I breathed again when no monetary reward followed the blessing of what looked like a jewel-encrusted dog-collar. Mrs Pring, though, made a wry comment when the local wine merchant delivered a crate of half bottles of champagne to the presbytery door marked URGENT. FOR THE ATTENTION OF THE REVEREND FR BOYD.

I could only naturally conclude that Miss Davenport had taken a fancy to me. But how could I be sure? This might be one of the lady's whimsies which Fr Duddleswell had spoken about. When at Mass I turned round to face the congregation to say *Dominus vobiscum*, 'The Lord be with you,' my eyes were drawn to hers as if by a magnet. She seemed to glow with expectancy. She put me off so much I kept stumbling over the words of the Mass and losing my place in the Missal.

Until then, my sexual fantasies had taken the shape of

being hotly pursued by dark and languorous females. They usually wore grass skirts, were garlanded with flowers, and had bare bosoms bumping up and down like bunches of grapes. Miss Davenport was hardly the kind of Judy whom Bishop O'Reilly had warned us against when he ordained us. She was more an embarrassment than a temptation.

At a guess she was twenty-five years my senior. Fur-wrapped and affluent, but flat-chested and not exactly beautiful. Her eyebrows, pencilled thin and blue, gave a haloed appearance to piercing brown eyes. There were lines on her forehead and down her neck, and her hair done up in a bun was streaked with grey. My conclusion was that it was silly and unfair to consider Miss Davenport some kind of *femme fatale* when perhaps she looked on me as a son.

True to my word, I handed over the envelopes to Fr Duddleswell who saw nothing incongruous in the scale of the offerings. His view was that if the good lady insisted on throwing her money around like snuff at a wake it was imperative the right people should be there to gather it up. I was fast becoming a financial asset to St Jude's if nothing else.

One morning the telephone rang while Fr Duddleswell was giving me instructions for the day. He answered it, gagged the mouthpiece, and whispered, ''Tis Miss Davenport for yourself, Father Neil.'

She sounded distressed. Her pet canary was unwell. I asked her if she had called in the vet. Yes, a specialist from Harley Street was with him at this moment, but what he really needed was a priest. I had so far spoken in ambiguous terms to spare Fr Duddleswell the bizarreness of the lady's conversation, but there was no way I could avoid asking, 'You did say your *canary*, Miss Davenport?'

Fr Duddleswell was not in the slightest put out at hearing

who was in need of my ministrations. 'Tut, tut,' he said softly, 'poor little creature.'

I advised Miss Davenport that if a Harley Street specialist was with him, her pet was in very capable hands. Fr Duddleswell signalled me to gag the receiver again before tapping my chest with his breviary and saying hoarsely, 'Is it a cooking apple you have in there, you great Gazebo of a man?'

I gathered I was expected to accede to Miss Davenport's request. I momentarily rebelled and played one more card. 'I'd be delighted to help, Miss Davenport'—Fr Duddleswell smirked—'but, you see, you live in All Saints parish, and really you ought to ask Monsignor Clarke to ...'

Fr Duddleswell's shaky fist was promptly over the mouthpiece. 'Jesus, Mary and Joseph,' he grinded out, 'tell the bloody lady you will bloody well be there in bloody double quick time.'

I only hoped he had a sound-proofed hand. I relayed the message to Miss Davenport in milder terms and replaced the receiver.

All the time I was changing from cassock to jacket, walking down the stairs, putting on my bicycle clips and wheeling out my bike, Fr Duddleswell was hovering over me, giving me a sermon on dropping once and for all this petty, trade union, demarcation-line mentality that was ruining the country and, instead, blessing the bloody canary and any other bloody thing necessary, as Jesus Himself would have done. I had never known him spit out so much blood.

I promised I would not disappoint the rich Miss Davenport and sped off as fast as two wheels would carry me.

The detached, white-pillared house was in a leafy square. It overlooked a small, fenced-in private park sparkling with well watered grass on a bright October morning. I rested and padlocked my bicycle against the black wrought-iron railings, next to a sign which read LE CASINO.

A French maid wished me *'Bonjour, mon père,'* and ushered me into the lounge where 'Madame is anxiously attending you.'

I was born an impressionist. I feel things but I do not always see them too clearly. I took in a Siamese cat sensually rubbing its side against heavy damask curtains. It was wearing the bejewelled collar I had blessed a few days before. I caught the distant barking of Miss Davenport's French poodles. I sensed I was in the presence of incongruous opulence. It reminded me of the set of a Molière play we had once put on at school.

Miss Davenport rose from her Chesterfield where she had been reclining as she contemplated with damp eyes the canary in its gilded cage. With ringed hand she set me beside her on the cool leather and took my hand. It was some time before she would give it back.

The symptom of the canary's sickness was that it refused every incitement to sing. 'I have had him as a bosom companion,' she murmured, 'for quite six months, Fr Boyd, and never has he denied me this pleasure before.'

'When did it ... he ...'

'Timmy is his name,' she said, clasping my hand more tightly as though the name somehow bound us closer together.

'When did Timmy sing last, Miss Davenport?'

'Yesterday evening.' She looked around her. 'Did you not bring your vestments, Fr Boyd?' She explained that she was expecting me to pray for Timmy's recovery and give him my sacerdotal blessing.

Fortunately, I had taken Holy Communion to a sick person that morning before Mass and I still had a small stole, a bottle of Holy Water and my Ritual in my pocket. Miss

Davenport thanked me for coming prepared and withdrew her hand reluctantly.

I put on my stole, white side up, and thumbed rapidly through the Ritual in search of a suitable benediction. The closest parallel I could find was the blessing of an aeroplane.

I raised my right hand over the little bird sitting sullenly on his perch and prepared to read the Latin formula.

'What is his name, Father?'

I was puzzled. 'You just told me his name was Timmy, Miss Davenport. I'm not baptizing him ...'

'No, he is baptized already, Father Boyd. I meant, what is Timmy's name in Latin so that I can recognize it when you utter it.'

'*Timotheus.*' I was thankful the canary had a simple Christian name and also that Miss Davenport's ignorance of Latin guaranteed she'd not realize my prayer had been written with a weightier sky-traveller in mind. At random moments during the prayer, I slowed down to say '*Timotheus*' at which Miss Davenport, who was kneeling reverently, bowed her head. At the end she said 'Amen.' Still no cheep from Timmy himself.

To complete the ceremony, I picked up the Holy Water sprinkler. It was simply a medicine bottle. The cork had been pierced to allow a few beads of water to escape when it was shaken over the sick. I aimed it at Timmy and began '*Benedicat te, Timotheus, omnipotens Deus ...*' As I jerked the bottle, the cork flew out and a stream of water went in Timmy's eye. Before the blessing was finished, the canary was in full voice.

Miss Davenport was ecstatic at so sudden a cure. She sat down at her bureau twittering something about not needing to call in that ineffectual 'médecin' from Harley Street and writing out a cheque. She sealed it in a pink envelope and gave it to me. WITH BOUNDLESS GRATITUDE, I read. 'Do you love cats, too, Father Boyd?' was her final question.

'We dislike the same things,' I replied diplomatically.

Outside the house, I was so incensed at being forced to make a fool of myself I tore up the envelope and stuffed the pieces in my back pocket. I cycled around town for half an hour, furious with Fr Duddleswell for casting me into the thin arms of a potty old girl merely to make a few extra bob for the coffers of St Jude's. When I had cooled down, I returned to the presbytery.

Fr Duddleswell met me at the back door. 'Miss Davenport rang,' he said, 'to make sure you returned ...'

I wheeled my bike into the yard and, without a word, walked past him up to my study. The atmosphere between us was strained until the next day when he visited my room to make peace.

'D'you know your trouble in all this, Father Neil?' I played the silent innocent. He lifted his spectacles on to his forehead and licked his lips noisily. 'You are a snob.'

I stiffened at the unexpected rebuke.

He raised his 'sermon fingers' at me, the first two on his right hand, and continued. 'Now be truthful with me, Father Neil. Had an old age pensioner called you to her flat in Stonehenge to bless her canary that had fallen ill with laryngitis, would you have obliged?' I nodded. He removed his fingers from before my nose. 'The rich are no different from the poor, Father Neil, except they have a lot more money, you follow?'

I apologized for sulking. Miss Davenport's distress at her canary's ailment was genuine enough. I should have sympathized more.

Fr Duddleswell coughed and said he would be obliged if I

39

would give him my signature. From his breast pocket he took out a cheque.

'Mrs Pring found the pieces in your waste-paper basket when she was cleaning this morning, Father Neil. I have taken the liberty of pasting it together, like.'

After I had signed THE REV. BOYD on the back, my resolution cracked. I turned it over to discover I had nearly thrown away twenty-five pounds.

When two days later, Miss Davenport begged me to bury her Siamese cat, Sleeky, who had been knocked over by a car I went prepared and in a more charitable frame of mind. I took my black bag with me and on the journey, with each revolution of the pedal, I told myself that Miss Davenport was only a poor little old lady with a pile of money.

Sleekius was interred with almost military honours and his mistress's many tears. I promised her I would say a Requiem Mass for the deceased on condition I did not have to announce the intention publicly from the pulpit.

Back at St Jude's, Fr Duddleswell summed it up by saying that after my success with Timmy it was best for my reputation as a healer that Sleeky had been 'killed beyond repair'.

Apart from magnetizing my eyes at every *Dominus vobiscum*, Miss Davenport did not trouble me again for another week. Then she phoned one Friday morning at around 11.30. Fr Duddleswell had been in my study for ninety minutes talking trivialities until I wondered if he would ever leave.

Miss Davenport asked if I could be at LE CASINO at eight. I was free, but I consulted my diary, trying to conjure up an excuse to stay at home. Fr Duddleswell's grimaces left me in no doubt that it was my duty to humour the good lady. Having heard me say yes, he left before I had replaced the receiver.

At the evening meal, Fr Duddleswell seemed miles away. He was reminiscing about obscure tribulations he had had to endure when he was a curate. Mrs Pring had cooked sausages and mash. In a moment of total vacancy, Fr Duddleswell served me a *single* sausage; hardly enough for one about to face the rigours of officiating at Miss Davenport's imediately afterwards. I asked for three more, buried them in a mound of mash and helped it down with a bottle of champagne. After that, plum pudding and custard. With a final flurry, I grimly drained two cups of Mrs Pring's tar-black tea.

'You are off, then, Father Neil? To Miss Davenport's is it?' I nodded. 'The best of luck, lad,' he said without his usual smile.

'Won't be long,' I called as I rode off. How was I to know that at Miss Davenport's there awaited me something more simple and more terrible than anything I could have imagined?

At the front door of LE CASINO, the maid and the chauffeur, presumably her husband, were on the point of leaving. The maid curtseyed to Miss Davenport, kissed her hand and said, '*Encore*, Madame, my sincerest *condoléances*.' Which member of the menagerie was dead now?

I walked in to find Madame attired not in black but in full evening dress.

In the hall, Miss Davenport monopolized my hand. The dining room door was open. Inside I could see the table tastefully dressed and lit by candlelight.

'I'm awfully sorry, Miss Davenport,' I stammered, 'if you're expecting guests I can come back tomorrow.'

'Only you, Father.'

O my God, I thought, do I have to dine with Miss Davenport by candlelight without any witnesses present?

Only then did I grasp the significance of the hour: eight o'clock. Dinner! *Damn!*

'You do have an appetite, Father?' purred my regal-looking hostess.

'Usually, Miss Davenport.' I was beginning to distinguish dangerous details in the candlelight. Her low cut dress, the pearl necklace, her hair brushing her shoulders and crowned with a kind of shimmering tiara. Taking my arm as well as my hand she propelled me to where the meal was waiting. Soft intimate music was being played in the background.

I helped her sit down before making my way to the other end and slumping down myself. I was surrounded by more cutlery and glass than I had ever had to deal with. Staring up at me malevolently were six large oysters bedded in crushed ice.

'You like oysters, Fr Boyd?'

Never having been that close to them before I was non-committal. 'Is there anyone who doesn't, Miss Davenport?' I had no idea how to eat the blessed things, or were you supposed to drink them?

I took a long time unfolding the starched table-napkin while keeping a sharp look-out for which piece of silver she would select. A tiny fork. She squeezed a lemon over the oyster and made a little slicing movement with her fork. She picked up the shell and, as it were, tossed the contents down her throat.

My aim was never very good and I was worried that oysters would not be companionable towards the *hors d'oeuvre* I had eaten with Fr Duddleswell. After the first throw I found my mouth full of a viscous substance like the raw white of an egg. It nearly made me vomit. My hostess's eyes were not yet accustomed to the light or she might have

suspected something. I went on chewing surreptitiously behind my table-napkin till I managed to swallow.

In front of me was a Menu printed on parchment paper in
silver lettering. It read:

> *Oysters*
>
> *Tournedos Béarnaise*
> *Potatoes Lyonnaise*
> *Tossed Green Salad with French Dressing*
>
> *Tarte aux Abricots Bourdaloue*
>
> *Cheese*
> *Fruit*
>
> *Coffee*

To drink there was *Château Haut-Brion* (1918) and *Haut-
Peyraguey*, and finally *Cognac Courvoisier*.

'Would you care to pour for the next course, Father?' Miss
Davenport pointed to the wines. I was glad to do anything
that afforded me some respite from another oyster.

As I rose, it occurred to me that I did not know which
wine was which or which to serve first. The white wine was
on ice and the red on the side-board.

'Have you any preferences, Miss Davenport?'

'Yes, on these occasions, always *Château Haut-Brion*
(1918).'

There was nothing for it. I chose the bottle resting on the
ice. In the nick of time I read *Haut-Peyraguey* on the label.
With considerable presence of mind, I half whispered, 'What
a splendid wine to follow, Miss Davenport.'

'I am so pleased you know your *Sauternes*, Father,' she
said.

I picked up the red and put my napkin under it as if it were a Stradivarius violin. Approaching my hostess I realized another distressing gap in my knowledge of etiquette. Into which glass should I pour the wine? Another hasty decision was forced on me, and with less fortunate results.

'That's the water glass, Father,' said Miss Davenport, touching my arm tenderly. She helped me by apologizing for the meagre light given by the candles.

Back at my place I looked down at the five-eyed monster on the platter in front of me. I noticed that the front of the Menu bore the initials *D.D.* and *N.B.*

'Fr Boyd,' said Miss Davenport as I was about to tackle another oyster, 'do you have a first name?'

I put down my fork. 'Yes, Miss Davenport.'

'May I be let in on your little secret?'

Since my initials were on the Menu and my full name was printed in capitals above my confessional, I did not mind revealing it.

'Neil? *Neil*.' She ran it over her tongue appreciatively like wine. 'Such an excellent vintage. It suits you. It *is* you. Now you have told me that your name is Neil, I could not conceive of you possessing any other name. I shall call my next Siamese Neil—if it is a boy, of course.' I acknowledged the compliment. 'May I, *dare* I, call you Neil?'

'I don't think Fr Duddleswell ...' I began as I directed another oyster towards my throat.

'Charles?' she said. I swallowed the oyster without difficulty. 'Ah, Charles would not begrudge me such an innocent pleasure.'

'Charles?' I managed to get out.

'I am Daisy.'

'I'm sure you are, Miss Davenport.'

'You see, dear Neil, I feel we have to be on Christian name

44

terms if I am to confess to you the story of my love.'

I stood up, seeing my first opportunity to escape that insupportable meal. 'Miss Davenport, you are a Catholic and I am a priest.'

'Daisy.'

Less forcefully I repeated my objection preceding it with 'Daisy.'

'It is *because* you are a priest, Neil, that I can tell you without inhibitions of my love for ...' I was about to stamp out when I heard the word 'Henri.'

'Henri. Monsieur le Comte. My first, my only love.'

I sat down as though I had been shot. It was only my ear Miss Davenport was wanting to grab, after all. It meant I would have to see the meal through to the bitter end. Miss Davenport was destined to be my *femme fatale* in a way the moralists had not envisaged when they advised, 'Never be alone with a woman, *Numquam solus cum sola.*'

As the meal progressed and the candle flame burned low I learned that Miss Davenport had met Monsieur le Comte in the Casino at Monte Carlo when she was seventeen. He was, *hélas*, a married man with a beautiful but boring wife, an ancient château on the Loire, and half a dozen children. It was a sad tale and it moved me deeply.

Miss Davenport, having despatched her *Tournedos Béarnaise* touched her mouth with her napkin. 'Rarely does it happen,' she whispered reverentially, 'that the perfect wine comes into being.' As she fingered the stem of her glass, the candlelight played upon the ruby contents and from them flashed a star with the brilliancy of Bethlehem's. 'Such marvellous blending of rain and sunlight is required, wind and soil, too, and perhaps the protecting curvature of some small hill. Celestial chemistry, Neil. Only such unique conditions can produce a *Château Haut-Brion* (1918) or a genius like

Bach—or a Monsieur le Comte.'

Count Henri must have been a veritable bouquet of a man, handsome, high principled, bronzed, most subtle in speech and elegant in dress. The culture of his palate was evidenced in our meal; it was his favourite. It was the meal he had chosen to eat with Daisy the evening they said good-bye.

My pity was equally divided between Miss Davenport's past sorrows and my present predicament. Even as she related her sad *histoire* she remained the perfect hostess, urging me to eat this and drink that. My bladder was filled to over-flowing.

I should have excused myself for a few moments and asked where the bathroom was. This, I felt quite reasonably, would have dampened her discourse. And afterwards, how could I return to my place as if nothing had happened, especially if the plumbing of the water closet was such that it left hissings and pipe reverberations? Like a fool, I decided to sit it out.

My eyes started to water with the discomfort, and when the candlelight caught them in its glow Miss Davenport took it as a sign of sympathy and rapport.

'It was passionate but pure, Neil,' she was saying. 'Only one such as you committed to *la vie célibataire* could possibly comprehend my heartache and the subsequent solitude.'

I did not know what time it was but it must have turned 11 o'clock, curfew hour at the presbytery. What if Fr Duddleswell, not realizing I was out, had bolted the door?

The strain was now intolerable. 'Miss Davenport.' I changed to 'Daisy' of my own accord to show the evening had not been wasted on me. 'Daisy, I have a confession to make to you.'

'Tell me, Neil.' There was a touch of drama in her voice.

'I'm feeling ill, Daisy.'

'Where, Neil?'

I did not want to put too fine a point upon it. 'In my stomach. Frightfully, frightfully ill.'

'Not the food, I hope?' she asked in some distress.

'I wasn't too well before I came, Miss Davenport. If you don't mind ...'

'A cognac before you go. It is so good for an upset stomach, as Henri used to say.'

To speed things up, I gulped down a small cognac, grabbed my hat from the hall and took my leave. I had the presence of mind to kiss her hand. 'Daisy, adieu.'

She was deeply moved and, fortunately for me, closed the door behind me immediately. I unchained my bicycle but was unable to lift my leg high enough to sit on the saddle. To avoid permanent injury I began to wheel my bike home. Then a flash of inspiration ignited by desperate need, I hailed a passing taxi.

The taxi came to a halt and the driver put his capped head out of the window and asked in puzzled tones, 'Trouble, Rev.?'

'Deep trouble,' I said.

'Puncture?'

'Almost.'

'Want me to take the bike an' all?'

I had opened the back door and was already dragging my bicycle in after me. I thanked God for the sensible design of the London taxi.

'First time I've ever had a bike for a fare,' called the driver good-naturedly over his shoulder. 'Where to, Guv.?' I gave the address. 'Roman Catholic, then, are you, Father?'

'Yes.'

The driver relaxed his hand on the wheel and half turned

round. 'My old woman's a Catholic. Could you tell me something, Rev.?'

'I can't tell you a thing,' I said, clasping myself where it hurt, 'please get us home quick.'

He slammed the glass partition between us with an 'O-bleeding-kay, if that's the way you want it,' and sped off through the city traffic like a maniac. Whenever he went through the red lights I gave him a special benediction. I prayed frantically that Fr Duddleswell had not bolted the door, otherwise I might have to pee against a lamp post.

The taxi jerked to a stop outside the presbytery. The driver touched the clock and said, 'And an extra threepence for your bleeding bike.' I handed him a pound note and told him to keep the change. I was not prepared to wait for it. I hoped the liberality of the tip would soften his attitude to the leaders of his wife's religion.

The front door was already ajar and Fr Duddleswell stood there against the light in dressing gown and slippers. He must have heard the familiar ticking over sound of the taxi. I expected a reprimand for being out after hours, but nothing of the sort. He merely pointed. 'Quick, up the wooden hill with you, Father Neil. The bathroom is free.' I left my bicycle in his charge and heaved myself heavenwards.

Ah, such simple, unsung ecstasies. Such blessed relief. Never had life seemed so sweet, so very sweet.

Outside the bathroom Fr Duddleswell was waiting with a bottle of Milk of Magnesia and a dessert spoon. I went with him into my study. 'At your age, Father Neil, you have to be more careful that the Jordan does not burst its banks.'

'She rang, then,' I said, collapsing into a chair.

'Who, Miss Davenport?'

'Yes.'

'No.' I had swigged three spoonfuls of the medicine before

48

it sank in that Fr Duddleswell knew my plight in some detail without being told.

'Monsieur le Comte,' he said.

'You know about him?'

From his pocket he drew a dog-eared Menu, a replica of the one on the table that evening except it was initialled *D.D.* and *C.D.*

'Charles,' I exploded.

'We have all to go through it the once, Father Neil. I did meself and so did me two curates before you. Take your ease and I will tell you about it.'

He had known tonight was the night because of the date, October 13th, the anniversary of Daisy's final farewell to Henri. The incidents with the pets were part of the usual build up to the banquet.

When I suggested that we should not make fools of ourselves for money, Fr Duddleswell looked hurt.

' 'Tis true, Father Neil, that in a couple of days I will receive a cheque for £500 for the Schools' Fund as has happened a trinity of times before. But as God is me witness I did it all for Daisy.'

It was news to me that anyone else had been involved apart from myself.

He went on to explain that Miss Davenport had renounced her beloved rather than break up his marriage. She had acted in strict obedience to the Church's law on marriage and divorce. With her purchasing power she could have bought out any half-baked Frenchman. The meal I had just shared was, in his view, a kind of eucharistic memorial of the last supper when Daisy sacrificed herself for her faith.

'You believe her story?' I asked.

'To speak the truth, I have not the faintest idea whether it happened like that or she imagined it. What matters is that 'tis real for her, you follow?—and the rich are especially worthy of a priest's consideration.' He slowly raised his head and dropped it. 'You see, lad, they cannot take refuge in the ultimate human illusion that money is the cure of every form of ill.'

I nodded, truly sorry for having misjudged both him and Daisy.

'One thing, Father,' I said in a more sober tone, 'you knew what was in store for me. Why did you let me eat that vast quantity of stodge beforehand?'

'Well, Father Neil, you had got so fractious over the mere blessing of a canary I thought you might opt out altogether, like. Besides, did I not try to let you off lightly by rationing you to a single sausage?' He stretched out his podgy hand in fellowship. 'No hard feelings, lad?'

But this time I could not forgive him. I was lurching back to the bathroom on a far more urgent errand.

Three

FR DUDDLESWELL IS DRUNK IN CHARGE

Mrs Pring was serving breakfast in a new bottle green dress and black patent leather shoes, a sure sign that today was her birthday.

I complimented her on her hair-do and presented her with a Parker pen. Fr Duddleswell's gifts were more exotic. The housekeeper's excitement mounted as she rummaged in the carrier bag he had placed on the window-ledge. A cameo brooch, a microlite table lamp for her bedside and, last, well wrapped up, a bottle of Gordon's gin.

'I don't know what to say,' she got out.

'If I had known it needed but a little gift to render you speechless, woman,' said Fr Duddleswell, 'I would have practised magnanimity towards you long ago.'

Instinctively I stood up and planted a kiss on Mrs Pring's plump cheek. That brought on the tears which Fr Duddleswell's remark was designed to check.

'Now, Mrs Pring,' he warned, 'I will not have you behaving here like a Jew in Babylon, else I will give you the full of me mouth, your twenty-first birthday or no.' I had never known him have such a blunt edge to his tongue. 'Now, wash that Ash Wednesday mug of yours, will you not? And be ready, mind, when your daughter comes to fetch you.'

At 9.30 a grey Morris Minor drew up at the back door. On hearing it, Fr Duddleswell bade me accompany him to the kitchen. Half a dozen cards were displayed on the mantel-piece and Mrs Pring was adding another from her daughter.

'Helen,' cried Fr Duddleswell delightedly.

'Uncle Charlie,' returned Helen, and she raced towards him with outstretched arms.

When the embrace was over, Fr Duddleswell introduced me to his 'niece'. Helen Phipps was in her early thirties, pretty, petite and smartly dressed.

'Father Neil,' said Fr Duddleswell, drawing himself up to his full five feet seven, 'is not this the beautifulest colleen that ever set foot in St Jude's?' I did not say no. 'Take that pair of sparkling eyes, now, those rosy lips. And those teeth, what are they if not Solomon's flock of even-shorn white sheep? Is she not living proof, Father Neil, that God Almighty can make a silk purse out of a sow's ear?'

'He's scrag end of mutton himself,' said Mrs Pring, stifling her real emotions, 'and he pretends he's fillet steak.' A few more tears escaped and glossed her cheek.

'Did you not hear me tell you,' said Fr Duddleswell stamping his foot, 'I will not have you dripping hot and cold in me kitchen.'

'*My* kitchen,' shouted back Mrs Pring, quite recovered all of a sudden, and Fr Duddleswell, as his costliest birthday gift to her, conceded the point. ' 'Tis worth more than double,' he said, 'so she takes her knuckles out of her eyes.'

After a few more minutes' banter and detailed instructions from Mrs Pring on how to heat up the stew for supper, Fr Duddleswell produced a two pound box of chocolates for the three grandchildren. Then a sharp, 'Be off with the both of you, and say a prayer to St Christopher, mind.'

That day we lunched at the Clinton Hotel. Fr Duddleswell told me how Mrs Pring had been with him 'the worst part of twenty years'. It had not hit me before that Helen, whom I had met for the first time that morning, must have been with her mother when Mrs Pring 'took up office'.

Every time my parish priest spoke of Helen his eyes shone. As the meal wore on he was quite voluble in her praises. It could be his two half pints of ale had something to do with it.

After coffee, he asked if I were ready for home. I had drunk my usual couple of glasses of wine. 'Certainly, Uncle Charlie,' I said. I thought my impertinence may have affected him because it was with difficulty that he rose to his feet.

Though drowsy, I noticed in the car that he kept blinking furiously, and once he leaned over the wheel to rub the windscreen with his sleeve as if it were misted up.

His erratic driving shook me out of my somnolence. I hung on to my seat with both hands and joined Mrs Pring and daughter in fervent prayers to St Christopher.

It was market day in the High Street. There Fr Duddleswell swerved and hit a greengrocer's stall. Fortunately, we had slowed to about five miles per hour, but the barrow collapsed instantly. Pyramids of apples, oranges, tomatoes and melons were tossed in all directions. Many burst and squelched under the tyres of buses and cars.

Fr Duddleswell braked in a daze, his face ashen and his knuckles white. As he clutched the wheel, he was shaking visibly.

A noisy crowd was gathering and the stall holder was cursing in colourful cockney as he tried to recover some of his fruit and veg.

Within thirty seconds a police car was on the scene and out stepped the two constables who had invaded Mrs Pring's kitchen on the night I couldn't sleep.

P.C. Winkworth and P.C. Richards, approaching slowly

from the front, recognized us immediately and exchanged a glance. Once more the senior of them started to take out his notebook.

He opened the door on Fr Duddleswell's side. 'Would you care to step outside for a moment, sir, and show me your driving licence?'

Fr Duddleswell heaved himself out and held on to the door to stop himself falling. 'I'm not feeling . . .' he began.

P.C. Winkworth sniffed sardonically through his small red nose. 'Been wetting your whistle, have you, sir?'

I leaned over and called out, 'Only two halves of ale, Officer.'

P.C. Richards, still sporting a black eye, poked his arm through the window and grabbing my shoulder, said, 'When we want a statement from you, we'll ask for it, *sir*.'

The stall holder, senses restored, pushed to the front of the crowd. He saw for the first time that it was Fr Duddleswell who had done the damage. 'Are you okay, Father?' he asked with concern.

'I am in no way wounded, thank you, Michael,' said Fr Duddleswell, grateful no doubt that the stall holder was one of the good people of his parish.

He summed up Fr Duddleswell's predicament in a flash and, having no love for the Law, he apologized for pushing his barrow too far into the road. 'I might 'ave caused you two Fathers to be involved in a ruddy accident.'

The two coppers took the hint, but P.C. Winkworth declared doggedly that they would have to run the older clergyman in on suspicion of being drunk while driving.

Since I couldn't drive, P.C. Richards radioed Control for a breakdown van to tow our car to the police compound. Then we were driven to the Station.

There again fortune smiled on us. The Sergeant on duty

was Patrick O'Hara. He touched his forelock in salute as we approached his desk attended by his two junior colleagues.

The reception area, with its pale blue walls, was as inhospitable as a public lavatory. 'I have not been to gaol,' muttered Fr Duddleswell, 'since me last game of Monopoly.'

'Drunk in charge,' asserted Black Eye.

'Is that so, now?' said Sergeant O'Hara, peering over an enormous nose. 'And which of the two reverend gentlemen would you be accusing of this heinous crime?'

'The short fat one,' growled P.C. Winkworth, aware of forces at work here beyond his comprehension.

The Sergeant persuaded the two constables to leave the matter with him for a few minutes while they bought themselves a well-earned cup of tea. After they had gone, with some reluctance, Sergeant O'Hara made no bones about it: when there was a conflict between the Law and the Gospel, it was his duty as a policeman to uphold the Gospel.

'There is not a word of truth to it, Paddy,' whispered Fr Duddleswell in a confessional tone of voice. 'I came over queer, I am telling you, but not even a girl-child could become inebriated on one pint of diluted ale. Must have been something I ate.'

Sergeant O'Hara broke the news to Fr Duddleswell that it was his sad duty to summon one of the doctors on their list. 'What would you say, Father, to being examined by a Dr Daley?'

In ten minutes, Dr Daley arrived in bulk. Beads of perspiration stood out on a pink head bald but for a narrow circlet of white hair. His eyes were more bloodshot than usual. A cigarette was wedged in the corner of his mouth. The smell of whisky preceded him as he advanced, humming for our benefit, 'When constabulary duty's to be done, to be done.'

Having listened with scant interest to the charge in the presence of the two constables, he asked the Sergeant to be allowed to examine the accused in the politeness of a cell.

The three of us sat round a table on which Dr Daley placed his black bag. 'Now, Charles,' he said, 'I hear it rumoured you have been drowning the shamrock, like.'

'A few sips of ale only, Donal. Barely enough to wet me tonsils.'

'I cannot smell any alcohol on your breath, Charles, that's for sure,' said Dr Daley, suppressing a burp.

'Donal,' said Fr Duddleswell, 'in all the years we have been acquainted, have you ever known me be guilty of foolishness?'

'Indeed I have not. I have confessed to you the same many a time,' said Dr Daley choking, 'and I have another assignation with you next Saturday night and all, when my hope is you will pity me as now I pity you.' He sighed audibly and tapped his waistcoated tummy. 'It shames me that when I'm in my cups, my brogue betrayeth me and I betray the Green.' Another heave of his broad chest. 'Sweet Jesus, but it is hard, Charles, mighty hard to mortify the meat.' He slowly shook his head. 'I have this thirst on me, you see, like a fire. It is stoked by quenching.'

He went mawkishly on about his shame at allowing himself to become over the years 'as round as a pickled onion and more entirely tonsured by time, Charles, than even yourself.'

At length, he emerged from his reverie to assure Fr Duddleswell he would vouch for the innocence of one who had never raised his hand at any man, saving in holy benediction. It was blasphemous to contemplate his reverence being brought before a hanging magistrate and having his licence endorsed or taken away.

Dr Daley opened his bag. A bottle clinked as he took out his stethoscope. Good, I thought, as he put it round his neck, at last the medical examination is about to begin. I was wrong. It had just ended. The doctor was walking briskly towards the door. He paused with his hand on the knob to ask, 'And why, Charles, do you think these constables are endeavouring to smirch your excellent good name?'

Fr Duddleswell staggered to his feet. He explained that they had burst into our house one night without a warrant screaming obscenities and Father Neil had bravely blacked the eye of one before the other kneed him in the unmentionables.

Dr Daley nodded sagely. 'That clears that up, then.' He flung the door open, pushed Fr Duddleswell ahead of him and proclaimed in the manner of Pontius Pilate, 'Look at this man. I can find nothing to charge him with.'

'But,' protested Black Eye, 'you haven't made him walk the gang-plank yet.'

'Nor have I, Constable,' said Dr Daley. 'Nor have I.' He gestured to a thin white line parallel to the wall and indicated to Fr Duddleswell that he should walk carefully.

'Father Neil,' whispered Fr Duddleswell in my ear, 'I never had much of a talent for treading the straight and narrow.'

I patted him on the back for luck and he followed the white line steadily enough until the end when he lurched to his right.

'There, what did we say?' called out Constable Winkworth, 'he's drunk.'

'He is as shober, shir,' said Dr Daley, 'as you or I. Watch me.' He gave a dramatic slow motion imitation of a tightrope walker that would have earned him half a dozen deaths.

Sergeant O'Hara was completely convinced. 'Well, lads,'

he said kindly to the constables, 'it seems as if we'll have to drop charges.'

Outside, Dr Daley expressed himself satisfied that justice had been seen to be done. He told Fr Duddleswell he was probably suffering from a bilious attack. Nothing that a good dose of salts wouldn't care. 'If not,' he said, 'pay me a visit at my surgery.'

He volunteered to give us a lift home but we preferred to walk and go on living. I phoned George Walker, a trusted parishioner, asking him to pick up Fr Duddleswell's car from the police compound and took 'the drunk' home in a taxi.

At the presbytery, Fr Duddleswell leaned on me as he went upstairs to his bedroom. When I left him, I heard him bumping into things. After that, silence.

He did not appear at tea, and as supper approached he banged on my wall. I found him propped up in bed. 'Everything keeps spinning round, Father Neil, like a catherine wheel,' he said, 'till the world turns white as the skirt of a poached egg.'

I ate the stew alone and waited anxiously for Mrs Pring's return. At 10 o'clock, she came in with Helen. She sensed that something was wrong and rushed upstairs leaving me to chat awhile across the kitchen table with Helen.

It was easy to talk to Helen. She told me that when she was in her early teens her mother couldn't make ends meet on a war widow's pension. Jobs were hard to come by during and after the Depression. Fr Duddleswell had given her mother employment and both of them a roof over their heads. 'I never knew my father,' she said simply, 'so Uncle Charlie was a kind of father to me.'

Helen had lived in presbyteries until she married Bill, a solicitor. 'He had to give a good account of himself to Uncle

Charlie, I can tell you,' she laughed. 'Uncle Charlie even pressurized him into becoming a Catholic. He didn't want any mixed marriage for "our Helen", he used to say, and for once Mum agreed with him.'

I felt sufficiently at ease to ask Helen why her mother and Fr Duddleswell were always at one another's throats. 'That's his way of showing her affection without competing with my father,' Helen replied. 'Once he said to me, "Helen, I only ridicule your mother so she realizes that in my eyes she is not beneath contempt." It slipped out really, Father, but I think he was trying to say that if he was merely polite to her as most priests are to their housekeepers he would not be respecting her as she deserved.'

It sounded to me more like an enigma than an explanation but just then Mrs Pring returned. 'A real puzzle,' she said. 'He has no temperature and he's not vomiting, and yet he feels terribly sick and dizzy. It's either biliousness or food poisoning.'

At the Clinton Hotel, he had eaten pork fillet whereas I had chosen lamb cutlets. The pork might have been off but that was unlikely in view of the Hotel's high standard of catering and the speed with which Fr Duddleswell had succumbed after lunch. Only time would tell what was really wrong with him.

For the next few days, I was Fr Duddleswell's constant companion. I assisted him at Mass. I made sure he didn't drop the chalice and I distributed Holy Communion for him.

' 'Tis a strange thing, Father Neil,' he said. 'Me head turns round faster when I am lying down than when I am standing up.' He was sleeping well enough provided he was propped up in bed, and his appetite was normal.

Mrs Pring decided that Fr D wasn't larking about this

time and insisted that Dr Daley give him a thorough examination. This was arranged for 8 p.m.

The doctor, smelling of peppermint, tapped and listened with his 'cruel Siberian stethoscope on a tropical chest', he shone a torch into his patient's eyes and ears. Afterwards, he delivered his diagnosis in one word: 'Labyrinthitis.'

'It sounds,' said Fr Duddleswell, 'as though I have a horned Minotaur prowling up and down inside me head.'

Dr Daley explained that it was not his head that was the trouble. Labyrinthitis is a virus infection of the inner ear which interferes with the balance mechanism. 'That's what I think anyhow,' he concluded.

'Do you not know for sure, Donal?'

'Dogma is your own business, Charles. I'm but a poor relation in the guessing game.'

In answer to how long it would last the doctor said, 'Ah, it is not so easy to heal the sick as to forgive sins. It usually clears up in about ten days. In the meanwhile, stay on the perpendicular as much as possible. Don't drink or drive until you get the all-clear, and get yourself a walking stick. It'll lengthen the odds on you falling over arsy-varsy.'

'I beg your pardon,' I said, not sure if I had heard correctly.

'I said I do not want our beloved P.P. pirouetting in the street like a drunken ballerina and falling bang on his bum.' My ears were in perfect working order.

The doctor prescribed tablets and promised to arrange for X-rays at the Sussex, one of the finest teaching hospitals in London, to verify his findings.

Three days later, Fr Duddleswell and I took a taxi to the Sussex. First, he was examined by Mr Taylor, a specialist who wore a kind of miner's lamp in the centre of his forehead. Fr Duddleswell complained that he was as non-committal as a canon lawyer. After that, a nurse escorted us to a room where another white coated gentleman made Fr Duddleswell lie on a bed and directed warm water from a nozzle into his ear.

Fr Duddleswell immediately noticed that pasted on the ceiling was 'a lewd photograph'. True enough, smiling down on us from on high was a picture of a young woman in a low cut dress. Fr Duddleswell interrupted proceedings to demand an explanation for the strange location of such filth in a National Health Hospital.

The doctor said that injecting water into his ear would cause his head to spin and the picture would revolve wildly. His job was to time with a stop-watch how long it takes the patient to recover normal vision.

'Never,' returned Fr Duddleswell, 'while that hussy *in impuris naturalibus* is leering down at me.' He closed his eyes firmly until they sent for a workman with a ladder to replace the pin-up with a picture of a Beefeater on duty outside the Tower of London.

Fr Duddleswell could only manage water in one ear. When the Beefeater finally came back into focus, he felt violently sick. 'Me stomach's bid goodbye to its cage,' he said, looking not white but green about the gills.

When he had recovered, I supported him downstairs to the X-ray room. 'Take your clothes off, please, sir,' said a West Indian nurse.

'I have not the slightest intention of peeling meself like a spud beneath the public gaze,' retorted Fr Duddleswell, waving his stick at her. ' 'Tis an X-ray I am here for, not a Turkish bath.'

According to the nurse, he only had to take off his spectacles, his upper garments as far as his vest and to step out of his shoes.

Mumbling something about Soho and striptease, and

being seen in 'the altogether' and not feeling like a human being at all without his clerical collar, he complied.

A doctor appeared and pointed to a kind of operating table. 'Help your old dad up there,' he said to me. 'Oh, and by the way, get rid of that lucky charm he's wearing round his neck.' Fr Duddleswell kissed his miraculous medal passionately and handed it to me for safe custody.

Once on the horizontal, he was strapped down to prevent him moving his head while being X-rayed. Just before the pictures were taken he summoned me to him and said out of the corner of his mouth, 'Tell me truly, Father Neil, d'you reckon I will make a tolerable Frankenstein?'

As he was putting his clothes back on I realized something else was wrong with him. Not only was he unsteady on his feet, he was wriggling violently from side to side like a snake sloughing off its skin.

'What's the matter, Father?'

' 'Tis the ultimate tragedy, Father Neil,' he confided. 'Me bloody collar stud has slipped down me back.'

I encouraged him to keep wriggling and the stud was bound to reappear at the bottom of a trouser leg. After three minutes of contortions it was clear I'd been too optimistic.

'I am afraid,' he said through clenched teeth, 'that the cursèd thing is stranded inside me Long Johns.'

I looked at him in surprise. The weather was still far too mild to justify him taking to his winter woollies.

'I was not aiming under any circumstances, you follow Father Neil? to parade up and down this hospital like Adam before the Fall.'

There was nothing for it but to locate the stud and work it downwards. I fingered it as far as his left calf, after which it would not budge. I asked the coloured nurse if she could lend me a pair of surgical scissors. The only pair she had

were the size of garden shears. I snipped a hole in the Long
Johns and Fr Duddleswell was happy again. 'Me curate has
just removed a worrying little abscess, nurse,' he explained.

As we were leaving, the nurse took me aside and advised
me to go straight home and put the 'poor old chap' to bed
with a hot water bottle and a couple of aspirins.

'Father Neil,' the poor old chap said to me the next morning,
'*you* will have to do it.' When I asked *what*, he replied that
his imitation of Boris Karloff had gone far enough. Because
he distrusted the shakiness of his hand he was now sporting a
five-day growth and ''tis against diocesan regulations to
show a chin as tufted as a billy goat's.'

I offered to shave him with my electric razor but he professed abhorrence of such new fangled gadgetry. He would
much rather use sand-paper.

He drew me to the bathroom and opened up the cabinet
where he stored his shaving gear. Out came a long, black
handled cut-throat razor, lethal looking.

'I can't, Father,' I stammered, 'I'm maladroit, you know
that.'

''Tis a scrubbish, mean man, so y'are, Father Neil.' I
acknowledged it. 'A soft, wet potato.' No description, I said,
ever suited me better.

Mrs Pring overheard us and volunteered for the job. The
equipment was set up in her kitchen. A Toby jug for the
soap mix was on the table and the leather strap hung from a
hook on the door. 'Keep stropping that razor, lad,' Fr
Duddleswell urged, 'unless 'tis sharp, 'twill cut me to rib-
bons.'

Mrs Pring sat him down on a straight backed dining room
chair and draped a towel round his neck so that he looked
like a criminal in the stocks. 'I'll never have a better op-

portunity,' she giggled. She removed his spectacles and asked him if he wished to be blindfolded. 'Any last requests, Fr D? Burial? Cremation?' Then she lathered him to his eyes.

I handed her the razor. She rubbed the edge lightly against her left index finger. 'Into Thy hands, O Lord,' he prayed. She made a scything movement in the air and expressed satisfaction that now Father Neil had given her the tools, she would finish the job.

'He was led,' intoned Fr Duddleswell, 'like a lamb to the slaughter.'

'And,' took up Mrs Pring, 'he opened not his mouth.'

'Neither *will* I, woman, provided you do not wave that thing around like a crazy Samurai.'

'Close it,' she warned, pointing the razor at his frothing mouth, and he obliged by closing his eyes, too.

For two minutes not a sound from Fr Duddleswell, only the crunch and scrape of the razor on his beard. 'Not so much of your lip, please, Samson,' rejoiced Mrs Pring, as she wiped the razor clean on a piece of tissue paper.

He only yelled once when she very slightly grazed his chin. 'Oh,' cried Mrs Pring, 'he's haemorrhaging. Father Neil, go fast and fetch Dr Daley to patch up his pimple.'

Her last great moment came as she was finishing off his upper lip. '*Alo-ong came a blackbird*,' she sang, '*and*'—zip— '*pe-ecked off his nose.*'

Fr Duddleswell rose unsteadily and walked off without a word. 'One thing, Father Neil,' Mrs Pring said to me with a wink which had more worry than humour in it, 'there's proof that you *can* get blood out of a stone.'

Mrs Pring did not take her day off that week. It showed how anxious she was about him. She gave me an envelope containing a ten shilling note 'for a Mass for Fr D' and she con-

fessed to saying not just the rosary, but the trimmings as well
for his recovery.

That evening I heard Fr Duddleswell groaning in his bedroom and went to see what was wrong. 'You will never believe this, lad,' he said, 'but now I have the bloody toothache.
Am I not stricken enough without fresh pains in me kneaders
and grinders?'

Mrs Pring's hearing was very acute. She was at his side in
an instant.

He turned a swollen cheek to me. 'Am I all the while to
have that bold woman on sentry duty at me door, Father
Neil, staring at me with both ears?'

Mrs Pring declared she would call the dentist first thing in
the morning and fix an appointment.

'If I am to die, Mrs Pring,' he said, upright against the
pillow, 'what is the purpose of me suffering first in the
dentist's chair?'

'Oh, Father,' I blurted out, 'surely you don't want to die
with a toothache'—at which they both laughed heartily.

Mrs Pring had her way and at 11 o'clock next morning Fr
Duddleswell was in the torturer's chair.

'Well, what is the verdict, Tom?' he said to the tall, thin,
slightly cross-eyed dentist who had examined him. 'Are you
about to shove your road digging equipment down me
throat, then?'

Tom Read lowered his white mask, bit the inside of his lip
and shook his head. 'It'll have to come out, Father.'

'Never! 'Tis me best ivory by far, the last of me wisdom
teeth.'

'I'll give you an injection for it, Father.'

'May be so, Tom,' said Fr Duddleswell, eyeing the long
syringe on the glass table top, 'but what will you give me for
the injection?'

As the young lady assistant prepared the instruments, Fr Duddleswell recounted briefly the course of his distintegration. Vertigo, being shaved by a woman, having to walk on his curate's arm, or with the aid of a walking stick, and now the last worthwhile tooth in his head about to bite the dust.

I closed my eyes at the point where Fr Duddleswell seemed to be swallowing the dentist's fist.

On our return, Mrs Pring immediately noticed the blood on Fr Duddleswell's lips. ' 'Tis nothing,' he said with merciful speed. 'I have only parted company till resurrection day with one of me teeth.'

Mrs Pring's rejoinder was instantaneous. 'That's one less for your Reverence to gnash in the Fire.'

He sat down and screwed his tongue into the blood filled cavity before turning to me. 'Father Neil, here am I, down on me luck like Job on his dunghill, and there is herself taunting me like Eliphaz the Temanite.'

Mrs Pring offered him sixpence for the tooth. 'If the mice don't want it,' she said, 'I can always leave it to the diocese as a first-class relic.'

Fr Duddleswell did not appear to mind the fact that his most valuable pair of scissors no longer matched. I think it was because he was so relieved the vertigo was disappearing. When he reclined in Tom Read's chair he had expected his head to start whirling faster than a dentist's drill. Instead, he felt no ill effects. 'What is left of me,' he prophesied, 'is on the mend.'

On the morning we returned to the Sussex Hospital to learn the results of his X-ray, Fr Duddleswell was in buoyant mood. He was sure he would be given a clean bill of health.

A stunning Korean nurse ushered us into a cubicle where we were asked to wait for Mr Taylor.

'Did you see that nurse, Father Neil?' he whistled. 'She is wearing black stockings in mourningful anticipation of me decease. Some of them have such sweet faces on 'em they would turn me head any day of the week.'

He went on to joke about the kind of funeral he looked forward to. A hearse drawn by six black horses. A solemn sung Requiem with the Bishop preaching a panegyric packed with the most beauteous mendacities. Trembling hands lowering him gently into the narrow house. The clergy chanting *In Paradisum*, tongue-in-cheek, and after, while their tears rolled down their cheeks into their whisky glasses, taking bets on who would be the next to go. And, of course, leading the procession in a black hair net, old Mrs Pring.

That was when we became aware of Mr Taylor's voice drifting in from an inner room. He was talking on the phone in a somewhat tired voice like a judge. At that distance, I could only pick up snatches of his conversation but I distinctly made out, 'Nice old chap ... Good job there's not the complication of wife and kids ... No doubt about it ... X-rays ... Tumour on the brain ... Yep, quite inoperable ... Should see Christmas through with a bit of luck ... No pain, no ... Shall I tell him or will you? ... Thanks, Doctor ... I'll see you get all the ...'

All this time Fr Duddleswell's grip was tightening on my arm. There flashed through my mind the memory of an old lady I had once met in hospital when I was a student. She was dying and she kept describing how her head was in a whirl and she felt as if she was falling, falling from great height.

The specialist entered and peered over the top of his half-moon spectacles. 'The Reverend Charles Duddleswell?' He was obviously surprised to see us sitting there.

'Yes,' I said.

As the specialist picked up the X-ray photographs, Fr Duddleswell sighed heavily, 'I heard your prognosis.'

'Prognosis?'

Fr Duddleswell said he didn't particularly want to leave the discussing of such sorrowful topics to his old friend Dr Daley. Mr Taylor sat there stunned for a moment trying to fathom out the situation.

He burst out with a laugh. 'I was gassing with a colleague on the phone and it wasn't about you, Mr Duddleswell. The worst you've got is a flea in the ear, so to speak.' He went on to explain that virus was a word used by the medical profession to cover up its almost total ignorance of the causes of many maladies. We were not interested.

A couple of minutes later, we shook hands with the doctor and went out, doing our best to support each other.

'Father Neil,' Fr Duddleswell said, while we waited for the taxi, 'that gentleman did not seem to realize that in the space of sixty seconds he had condemned me to death and reprieved me. Did you not hear him laugh?' And after a few moments of reflection, ' 'Tis strange how sadness and hilarity grow from the same stem like roses and thorns.'

Mrs Pring was waiting on the doorstep to check up on the efficacy of her Mass stipend. Her first sight of us could hardly have increased her hopes. We were both looking white and shaken as we stepped out of the taxi.

To Mrs Pring's enquiry, Fr Duddleswell replied with his usual delayed humour, ' 'Tis bad news, I am afraid.' Before he could conclude with, 'I am going to live,' I was stooping down to pick the housekeeper off the floor. Fortunately, she had fallen without banging her head.

I carried her to Fr Duddleswell's study, settled her in a

chair and ran to the kitchen for a glass of water. When I got back, she was already regaining consciousness. She was saying, 'Oh my head. Everything's spinning round and round.'

Fr Duddleswell said he knew how she felt.

'I'll look after you, Father dear,' she kept repeating, 'I'll look after you.'

Fr Duddleswell tried to break it gently to her that she might have a long and arduous job ahead.

'You *are* going to die, Father D?' she asked suspiciously, and she would not be fobbed off with another sip of water which was all he offered her for an answer.

I took the glass from him and stooped over Mrs Pring to make her drink but she was so outraged at his deception that she knocked me sideways. As I lifted my head, I cracked it on the stone mantelpiece right in the tender spot which had blacked the policeman's eye. There was an explosion of white light inside my skull and I sank down slowly on the carpet. When I opened my eyes, there were the three of us in a circle, clasping our heads.

Fr Duddleswell held out his hands to us guiltily. *'Ring-a ring of roses?'*

Mrs Pring pushed his hand aside. 'You are a fraud,' she cried. 'Do you hear me, Father D?'

'Mrs P,' he said, breathing heavily through his nose, 'I could hear you in me deafest ear.'

'A fraud. A fraud.'

'Be careful, woman,' he said menacingly, 'or I will raise these hands to you with the fingers hid.'

I had made my exit and bathed my bump in the bathroom a long while before the argument downstairs had ceased.

Four

THE NOVEMBER BLUES

The sermon began: ''Twas fifteen hundred long years ago when Edwin King of the Anglo Saxons was betwixt and between whether to receive the Christian missionaries into his kingdom.'

The sermon was being delivered in my room. 'At a banquet, one of the King's nobles arose and said, "Sire, this life compared with the life to come reminds me of one of the winter feasts which you partake of with your generals and ministers of state." '

The sermon was being given to me alone. By Mrs Pring. ' "Imagine, me dear people," says the nobleman to his King, "the snowy cold without, the blazing hearth within. Driven by the storm, a tiny threadbare sparrow enters at one door and flies in a flurry of delight around the great hall before making his way out the other." '

At this point, Mrs Pring's congregation doubled. Fr Duddleswell entered silent as a bird, and stood beside her. ' "No chill does that wee sparrow feel while he is with us, Sire. But short is his hour of warmth and contentment here. Then out flies he again into the raging tempest and the dreaded dark." '

Here Mrs Pring raised her sermon fingers solemnly. ' "Brief is man's life, Sire, as is the sparrow's." '

In chorus with the preacher, Fr Duddleswell declaimed, ' "We are as ignorant of the state which preceded our life as of that which follows it." '

As Mrs Pring tailed off in surprise, Fr Duddleswell continued quietly, ' "Therefore do I feel, Sire, that if this new faith can give us more certainty than we now have, it deserves to be believed." '

After a strange lull, Fr Duddleswell said, ' 'Tis a mighty fine sermon you preach, woman.' There was not a trace of sarcasm in his voice.

Mrs Pring had forewarned me that as Mary's month of October was passing Fr Duddleswell was due for his usual fit of the November blues. November is the month of prayer for the souls in Purgatory. The purple vestments, she maintained, darkened his soul like black frost on the window pane.

' 'Twill be no ordinary November for me,' he said out of her hearing. His recent experience at the hospital had, he swore, completely refashioned him. He had examined his conscience in so far as it would stand still long enough and learned a few home truths about himself.

'Just being told you are going to die, Father Neil, is sufficient to kill you. And did I accept it? Indeed, I did not. No act of contrition. No *In manus tuas, Domine. E contra*, me faith flew into fragments and there stood I, knock-kneed and thrilled with fear. I could only picture meself stretched out like a sardine and carried on four black shoulders.' He plucked three times at his breast like the strings of a double bass and sighed. 'I always knew I was mortal, like, but not till that black day, that *dies irae*, did it so much as occur to me that I was going to die.'

I sensed that as this was an oration it would be foolish of me to interrupt.

'There is worse to come, Father Neil. When the specialist told me someone else is doomed to die instead of me, I rejoiced like a heretic when the faggots went out. And though this unknown had no kith and kin to assist him through his last days I did not think even to ask for his name and address.' When I said nothing, he added, 'Not that they would have given them to me, mind.'

He slowly rose and crossed to the fire. There he sank down on his haunches and picked up a lump of coal and said:

> 'I sat on me hunkers
> I looked through me peepers
> I saw the dead buryin' the livin''

After which he dropped the coal on to the hungry flame. 'In my case, Father Neil,' he said, rising, 'growing old is like driving backwards down a long, dark tunnel. You think you are seeing further when you are only seeing less.'

I stammered something about not judging oneself too harshly and leaning on the forgiveness of Christ, but he had not quite finished. He had decided that his life was sodden with deviousness and uncharity. He apologized for his past misdeeds and assured me from his heart that he was about to turn over a new leaf.

As October drew to its close, many other old leaves started to turn as they tumbled in golden showers to the ground. The weather was chilly and when I cycled on my early morning rounds to distribute Communion to the sick there was a mist sometimes high on the tower blocks and in the cul-de-sacs. Mrs Pring bustled about lighting fires before breakfast 'to warm and content my two wee sparrows.'

Fr Duddleswell kept his word. Whenever Mrs Pring tried to rile him, she found him lock-jawed. There he sat in a daunting silence. He gritted and bared his teeth in a passable imitation of a grinning skeleton.

'Ah, Father Neil,' said Mrs Pring, 'at least he died a happy death. Has his Reverence yet reached that driving-back-wards-down-a-long-black-tunnel bit?'

He saved his remark for when she had left the room. 'Women have the advantage over us, you see, Father Neil. They have an inexhaustible fund of ignorance to draw on.' He meant this not as an insult but as a plain statement of fact.

I was the uncharitable one. I had cut back Mrs Rollings' instructions to once a fortnight so that my wounds would have a chance to heal.

That Wednesday she came clutching a copy of *The Watchtower* which a Jehovah's Witness had put through her letter-box. My heart soared for a moment at the possibility of her embracing an alien faith and then crash-landed when she said she simply wanted me to answer all their accusations against the Catholics.

The magazine had gone to town on Indulgences. I explained to my only convert—forced on me by Fr Duddleswell—that after forgiveness there remains the punishment due to sins. An Indulgence is a remission of the punishment which a holy soul in Purgatory would otherwise have to suffer.

Where did this remission come from? From the infinite treasury of Christ's merits and those of his saints. Yes, Mrs Rollings, that's why the Pope grants so many Indulgences and, yes, Mrs Rollings, only Catholics out of all mankind are eligible for them. And the days in question, Mrs Rollings, refer to the days which the early Christians spent in harsh penitential exercises and which have been commuted in recent times to prayers and good works.

'So all these lies are true, then,' she said. I asked her to

74

instance some of their calumnies so I might judge for myself.

'*The Watchtower* says,' she answered, 'that for a single Mass in San Francisco there was once an Indulgence attached of 32,310 years 10 days and 6 hours.' I blinked in disbelief at the sheer crudity of the fabricated figures.

'Is that more or less than a plenary Indulgence, Father?' I confessed I had no idea.

She proceeded to read for my benefit how Spaniards at five-pence a person used to pay £200,000 a year to qualify for Indulgences and how the first plenary was given by the Pope to pious Crusaders for slaughtering the Turks.

I asked caustically if the author of the scurrilous article quoted any sources. 'Yes, Father,' she said, and mentioned *A History Of The Church* by a famous Jesuit historian.

I let her ramble on, hoping she would not notice my own Papal Indulgence resplendent in its frame on the wall above her head. It entitled me to a plenary Indulgence at the moment of death provided I was in a state of grace, prayed for the Pope's intention and uttered the holy name of Jesus. Dying is bound to be a busy time.

'By wearing a scapular of the Immaculate Conception,' Mrs Rollings continued, 'a Catholic can obtain 433 plenary Indulgences and lots of partial ones.'

I could not let that pass. 'Authorities, please,' I demanded. She stumbled over the name, 'Alphonsus ... and something that looks like "liquorice".'

'Liguori?' I said and spelt it.

'That's right, Father.'

St Alphonsus is a doctor of the Church but I did not tell her that. I made a resolution not to intervene again.

'The Pope in a Jubilee year grants not merely a plenary but a *most* plenary Indulgence.' She paused and lifted her eyes from the page. 'Why should Catholics need more than a plenary, Father?' I shook my head. 'And if,' she reasoned, 'you can earn, say, a million days of Indulgences every twenty-four hours just by saying prayers, that's not very fair on the early Christians, is it?' I felt it was not for a curate to settle issues of that magnitude. 'After all, Father, the early Christians had to scourge themselves for months on end for their pardon, and Christians today only have to recite the rosary.'

I only dimly heard her after that. Her theme was the folly of Catholics believing that souls, which are spiritual, can burn in Purgatory, and the pluck of Martin Luther, and Pope Leo X rebuilding St Peter's in Rome on the proceeds of the sale of Indulgences.

Did I have to be condemned to death and reprieved like Fr Duddleswell before I could learn to love everyone?

At supper, I chanced to say I had been talking to Mrs Rollings about Indulgences. Fr Duddleswell congratulated me on preparing for November and asked if I had told her the story of Sixtus IV's visit to the Franciscan nuns at Foligno in 1476.

'No, Father Neil? Well, now, perhaps you did not realize yourself how the Pope gave the good sisters a plenary In- dulgence for the coming Feast of the Virgin. But the Holy Ghost moved him to give them something special.' I was expecting the Pope to grant the nuns a most plenary Indulg- ence. 'Pope Sixtus said, "Sisters, I give you full immunity from your guilt *and* your punishment every time you go to confession." '

'Fantastic,' I said.

Fr Duddleswell smiled. 'The Cardinals present had the same reaction, Father Neil. "*Every* time, Holy Father?" they gasped. His Holiness put his old hand to his heart and said, "Yes, I give these lovely sisters everything I have, like." And what then, Father Neil? The Cardinals all went down on their knees pleading, "Us as well, Holy Father, us as well." "All right," said His Holiness, "you as well."' Fr Duddleswell's eyes were glistening. 'Such a tender tale,' he said. 'I love it, indeed I do.'

I repeated one or two of the details Mrs Rollings had read from *The Watchtower*. Before I could quote the references Fr Duddleswell had drawn in a deep breath and exhaled it to dismiss the Church's accusers in a single satisfying word: 'Bigots!'

Halloween and the Feast of All Saints did nothing to lift his spirits. No more joyful songs from his gramophone. Even at Mass on All Saints Day he preached about another sparrow that rubbed its beak upon a mountain top. Every thousand years another bird of the same family followed suit. 'And when eventually, me dear people, that mighty heap was levelled to the ground, the first moment of eternity had scarcely begun.'

On November 2nd, the Feast of All Souls, he revived. Up at the crack of dawn, he popped in and out of church, praying for the departed. He celebrated each of his three Requiem Masses on the trot with lugubrious glee, pausing only to point out to his congregations that if they recited six *Paters*, *Aves* and *Glorias* and prayed for the Holy Father's intention 'a holy soul will obtain a plenary Indulgence and be freed forthwith from the pangs of Purgatory.'

My Masses followed, and after breakfast we spent the morning freeing the dead, *toties quoties*, a soul a visit, so to speak. One gulp of fresh air at the church door was sufficient to mark off one visit from another. Owing to the speed with which Fr Duddleswell prayed, by my reckoning he helped two dozen more holy souls than I to freedom. Perhaps mine,

I consoled myself, had been the greater sinners.

We were visiting with the Blessed Sacrament again after lunch when we spotted a shifty looking character in a brown mackintosh reading the notices pinned to the church door.

'Take a close look at Pinky Weston,' Fr Duddleswell whispered.

In the presbytery, he told me I had just seen my first Rapper. Someone who raps on doors to find out if the tenants have anything of value they are prepared to part with. Rappers are often ignoramuses which is why they mostly work in cahoots with antique dealers.

'I see,' I said, though it was only through a glass darkly.

Rappers, he told me, peep through windows hoping to find a bargain. They team up with window cleaners, interior decorators, meter readers, with anyone in fact who will give them a nod and a wink when they come across something that looks like an antique. It might be furniture, silver, pottery or glass.

Pinky Weston had a special reason for reading the notices at the back of our church. A Requiem Mass alerts him to look up the deceased's address in the Electoral Register. He visits the house before the corpse is cold, hoping a destitute widow will part with an item of value for a pittance if only to pay for the funeral.

Fr Duddleswell reported the rumour that when Pinky's offer on, say, a piece of pottery is refused, he sometimes fingers it and cracks it.

My surprise provoked Fr Duddleswell to say, 'He cracks it expertly, apologizes for the little "accident", and out of the kindness of his heart repeats his original offer. Most times the owner says he can have it now and good riddance. Pinky takes it to his dealer who fixes it so you cannot see the join. Well, what d'you say to that, Father Neil?'

'It's wrong, Father.'

'God's holy Mother, lad, 'tis bloody facinorous, so 'tis.'

'Very wrong,' I said heatedly.

I expected to be sent back into church to release a few more holy souls but the sight of Pinky Weston had turned his attention to other matters. He invited me, instead, to accompany him by underground train to the antique market in Portobello Road.

Above the roar and rattle of the train he told me how their family house in Bath, and later the one in Portobello Road, had been of great beauty. 'Full of it,' he repeated with a yell. 'Can you *hear* me? *Can you ...*'

I nodded.

I enjoyed the chatter and bustle of the cosmopolitan crowd in Portobello Road. Pigeons, like dun-coloured Holy Ghosts, pecked away at scraps on the pavement. Chestnuts were being roasted on braziers. With Bonfire Night only three days off, children stood beside stuffed scarecrows piping out, 'Penny for the Guy.' We sifted through bric-à-brac on the stalls and flattened our noses against shop windows.

He taught me about Hepplewhite armchairs, when the Sheraton period was, and once he called out, 'Look, Father Neil, a genuine Queen Anne chest of drawers dating from 1705.' I, who couldn't tell whether a woman was twenty-five or thirty-five, was terribly impressed.

We were passing a shop pasted with notices UNDER NEW MANAGEMENT when a middle-aged couple emerged. The lady wore a bright, flowered dress and butterfly-winged glasses. She tossed her blue-rinsed head derisively at the remains of a chair in the window and called to her husband who had a camera round his neck, 'Chuck, what a goddam load of junk.'

'Ten pounds for that *thing*,' said Chuck, tugging on his camera strap.

'What's that in dollars, honey?'

'A helluva lot,' grunted Chuck. 'Back home in New York, the garbage collectors would charge to take it away.'

Fr Duddleswell seized my arm and dragged me after him. Twenty yards further on, he released me and said, 'Did you hear that, Father Neil?'

'Americans,' I began, 'coming over here and ...'

'Shut your mouth. I mean, Father Neil, listen to what I am telling you. That "thing" is a bloody Chippendale.' I was about to say the chair was without a seat when I remembered that the Venus de Milo didn't have any arms and nobody seemed to mind.

'Now, hear me, Father Neil, this is what we are about to do.'

Five minutes later, we were inside the shop admiring a statue, two and a half feet high, of the Madonna and Child.

'Would you suppose,' said Fr Duddleswell in his preaching voice, 'that Mrs Pring would like to have this?'

Before I could reply, a young assistant in jeans had pushed his hair out of his eyes to enquire if he could be of help.

After some sales patter about the statue's age, its haunting beauty, the beechwood of which it was carved, its Flemish origin, he said that for us the price was £250.

Fr Duddleswell blinked, removed his spectacles and breathed on them carefully like the risen Jesus on the Apostles. He said, as he rubbed away the mist, that he thought the young gentleman had told him the statue was very old. A brand new one would surely be cheaper.

'How much did you want to spend on this lady, Guv?' the assistant sniffed.

'About five pounds,' answered Fr Duddleswell, 'maybe six.'

'What's wrong with a fountain pen?' said the assistant before retiring to an inner room where he doubtless elaborated his suggestion to a young woman in slacks who was manicuring her nails.

We moved towards the door. Fr Duddleswell half opened it and called to the young man, 'Could I perhaps have that old chair in the window for a fiver?'

The assistant, without looking up, said, 'Ninety quid.' I was thinking the Americans had got it wrong when the lad added, 'But since it's opening day you can have it for nine.'

Fr Duddleswell opened the door wider before asking me if Mrs Pring would care for that. 'Could be,' I said.

'You would not take six, I suppose?' asked Fr Duddleswell.

The young man wrenched his eyes away from his girl. 'Seven pounds ten,' he said, 'and that's my final offer.'

Grudgingly, Fr Duddleswell re-entered the shop. 'Take a cheque?'

'Cash.' And the deal was closed. 'Sorry I can't wrap it,' was the assistant's last audible irony.

Fr Duddleswell was in raptures. At breakneck speed, he sucked me in his wake until we reached DUDDLESWELL'S, formerly his father's business. Fred Dobie, the proprietor, greeted us with a smile. 'Going that way?' he asked, pointing to the railway bridge where secondhand stuff was for sale. Then, 'Good God, Fr Duddleswell, a Chippy.'

Fr Duddleswell told him how he had acquired it and, after some hard bargaining, handed over the chair in exchange for fifty pounds. Cash.

'Now,' said Fr Duddleswell to me, 'I will buy you a cup of tay.'

In the café I insisted on paying for the teas and two doughnuts. He noticed that the chap at the counter had charged me tuppence too much and refused on principle to waive the excess fare.

I ate and drank in silence while he tried to convince me that he had not diddled the vendor; talent in recognizing *objets d'art* is what the antique trade is all about. Portobello Road would close tomorrow if people did business in any other way. The chair did not even have a seat to it. Fred Dobie was likely congratulating himself this very minute on putting one over on *him*.

My silence was more telling than any counter-argument. Gradually, he was reduced to disconnected phrases like, 'Turning over a new leaf', 'no deviousness and no uncharity', 'poor young things just starting out in the trade', and 'on November 2nd when I should have been releasing holy souls'.

His tea was untouched when he jumped up and marched out of the café. I followed him back to the shop. He told the startled young man what was what, wrote him out a cheque for £20 'to more or less split the difference', assuring him that his signature was genuine, and left.

The young man came running after him with the statue of the Madonna and Child. 'I'm grateful, truly grateful,' he said. 'Please take this as a gift for your lady friend.'

I was staggered at such generosity. 'Virtue is rewarded.' I crowed, when the young man was back inside his shop chatting up his girl.

'Do not be such a bloody fool, Father Neil,' he snarled. 'Nobody here gives you a handful of water for nothing.'

'A fake, Father?'

He nodded. 'At least 'twill never suffer from woodworm.'

'Plaster?'

Another nod. 'Woolworth's could not sell it for sixpence. Still, I reckon Mrs Pring will prefer it to a Chippendale that is as open as a navvy's toilet.' He handed the statue to me as if it was more than his reputation was worth to be seen in its company.

In Pembroke Road, seeing a single leaf floating down from a sycamore tree, he recited something about angel hosts that fall *'Thick as autumnal leaves that strow the brooks/In Vallombrosa.'*

His continuing purpose of amendment impressed me. If only it had not brought upon him another fit of the November blues.

On the way home it was all *Ecclesiastes* and *Omar Khayyám*. *'Vanity of vanities'* followed by *'Alas that Spring should vanish with the Rose'*. The only interlude was when we stopped at a Games Shop in the High Street. Fr Duddleswell ordered five pounds worth of assorted fireworks to be delivered to the orphanage for Guy Fawkes Day, November 5th.

At the presbytery door we were met by Mrs Pring. 'I'm glad you're back, Fr D. Someone just phoned to say Jack Dodson is sinking.'

Fr Duddleswell snatched the statue from me, placed it in her arms and rushed to collect the holy oils. Mrs Pring called out over the Virgin's crowned head that he should wear his overcoat against the cold, but he was already on his way. 'Take care of the confessions for me, Father Neil, in case I should be late.'

I did duty for him in the confessional and ate supper alone. My worries grew when curfew hour arrived and still no sign of him. At 11.15, Mrs Pring put a thermos flask in his study and retired for the night.

At nearly midnight, Fr Duddleswell came in panting furiously. He charged past me as I stood at the foot of the stairs saying, 'Tell you about it later.' I could hear him unbolting the church door.

In two minutes the bolts clanged to, and he reappeared. In his study he frantically unscrewed the top of the thermos flask and poured himself a cup of Ovaltine. He had taken one sip when the clock on his shelf chimed 'the Mephistophelean hour'. He put his drink down disappointedly. He could drink no more if he was to celebrate Mass the next morning.

I was concerned about him. He had not eaten or drunk a thing since lunch and not even a drop of water would pass his lips until after his second Sunday Mass at 10 o'clock.

I apologized for having ruined his tea. ' 'Tis of no consequence, Father Neil,' he said gallantly. 'This afternoon, you saved me from further deviousness and uncharity. I am much obliged to you.'

I asked about Mr Dodson. 'He passed over at 10.30.' My parish priest looked tired and sad. ' "*The Leaves of Life keep falling one by one.*" ' He rubbed his eyes beneath his spectacles. 'I stayed to console the widow, like, on this her longest day. Ah, for her to be single-bedded after all these years. 'Tis enough to make an onion weep. No man at night to snug her and melt her with his breath.' Then a thought cheered him up a bit. 'Went off in style, though, did old Jack. It happened well to him. The last rites. He had it all, including the Papal Blessing. A very healthy death. Most likely he went straight home to God on angels' wings.'

Since Mr Dodson had obtained a plenary Indulgence from the Pope, why had Fr Duddleswell rushed into the church before All Souls' Day was over to get him another?

He read me. ' 'Twas to make sure, like.'

On Monday morning at 10.00, we set off together to comfort

the widow Dodson. On our walk, Fr Duddleswell expounded his views on Purgatory, the Catholics' half-way house to Heaven.

'The trouble with Protestant theologians, Father Neil, is they have no imagination. 'Tis their mistaken opinion that the bereaved like to think of their loved ones being taken immediately to Paradise.'

My reaction must have put me among the Protestants. 'When you lose someone you love,' he explained, 'you experience the overpowering need to comfort them. 'Tis hard indeed to picture the dead as blissfully content while you are still shattered and torn by the losing of them. There must be attunement betwixt living and dead, you follow? The Church's teaching on Purgatory takes account of this.' His view was that when the sorrows of the bereaved ease off and they leave *their* Purgatory then they are ready to feel that their dead have entered the joys of Heaven.

'What about the plenary Indulgence for the dead?' I asked.

'The faithful believe it and they do not believe it,' he said, which made the faithful seem as devious as himself.

The Dodsons lived in a prefab, that single story, factory-built house, lowered into position almost in one piece.

Mrs Dodson, white-haired and almost worn away to nothing by time, was touched by our visit. 'Come in, Fathers,' she said, 'while I make ye a cup of tea.'

Fr Duddleswell took her right forearm, pressed it tightly and simply said, 'Mary.'

Mrs Dodson put the kettle on the hob. While waiting for it to boil, she reminisced. Fifty-three years they had been together. God was good to let them see in the Gold.

'You'll never believe it, Fathers,' she confided, 'but when we wed, we couldn't afford a ring. So I went to the haberdasher's and bought myself a brass curtain hook. One farthing it cost.'

That hook had lasted fifty years when they bought each other a fourteen carat gold ring. 'His was engraved FOR MY DARLING JACK and mine has FOR MY DARLING MARY. I could have kept his, Fathers,' she said, wiping away a tear, 'but I thought it'd be nice if he wore it to Heaven.'

'A wise fellow, your Jack, Mary,' Fr Duddleswell put in hastily, 'arranging to go on the most propitious day of the year, All Souls, when Purgatory is cleaned out.'

'God's help is nearer than the door,' she said. As she made the tea she explained that out of their savings she was paying for a splendid funeral. 'He didn't want to go owing nobody nothing, Fathers.' The money even ran to a solid oak coffin.

'That's nice,' I said for something to say.

We sat sipping our tea until Fr Duddleswell picked up a large, pitted silver pot from the sideboard. 'How interesting,' he said with a curious nostalgic smile, 'how *very* interesting. Mary, did you know ...?'

The doorbell interrupted him. Probably a neighbour calling to offer sympathy. When Mrs Dodson opened the door, we heard a simpering voice say, 'Mrs Dodson?'

'Yes.'

'I was a close friend of your husband.'

The caller's name was Philip Weston. 'But friends of mine like your James call me Pinky.'

Father Duddleswell confided to me, 'That sharper must have the periscopic eyes of a toad.'

Mrs Dodson had to admit that her Jack had never mentioned him but she thanked him for the courtesy of his call.

'I used to have the odd drink with Jack in the local.'

Mrs Dodson said it must have been a long time ago because he had been bed-ridden for the last ten years. Pinky Weston conceded it was a long time ago. 'But you don't forget easy an old crony like Jack Dodson.'

Mrs Dodson was unwilling to let Pinky in until Fr Duddleswell called out, ''Tis all right, Mary, we are just about to take our leave.'

Pinky Weston's flat white face looked as if it were permanently pressed against a windowpane. Fr Duddleswell took no notice of him. Still with the pot in his hand, he said, 'As I was telling you, Mary, I am very intrigued by this pot.'

'My granma gave it me years ago,' said Mary. '*Her* granny, I believe, gave it to *her*.'

Fr Duddleswell smiled broadly. 'That accounts for it, then. My own father, God rest him, had one like this. Elizabethan silver.' When Mary expressed surprise at it being real silver, he said that the coating was worn off and perhaps she didn't realize that antiques are often worth considerably less when they are re-silvered.

Patrick Duddleswell Senior had sold his for £95. 'Mark you, Mary, 'twould be worth every penny of £200 were it up for sale today.' He pointed to indentations on the lid. 'There, it looks as if a fork has pressed down on the metal. Tiger marks.'

It seemed to me that Fr Duddleswell had cleverly warned Mary not to part with a family treasure. Pinky Weston must also have known that if he swindled the old widow he would have to answer for it to the Church.

At the door, Fr Duddleswell said, 'Keep in mind the old saying, Mary: "The three most beautiful things in the world are a ship under sail, a tree in bloom and a holy man on his death-bed."' Mrs Dodson half-smiled and half-cried. 'Oh, and by the way, Mary, which undertaker have you settled on?'

'Bottesford's,' she said.

I apologized for making no contribution to the visit. 'You are wrong,' he returned. 'You said but little but you said it well. Times there are, Father Neil, when words spoil meanings. 'Tis pitiful but when the deer of their woods has departed, what can you do but grasp them with kindness?'

He fell into a reverie, only coming out of it from time to time to utter the name Bottesford. He clicked his fingers and a few minutes later we were on the doorstep of Bottesford's Funeral Parlour.

I had not seen the proprietor since he ran out of the church some weeks earlier. He was fat—Fr Duddleswell said his hand was too kind to his mouth—and he wore an atrocious ginger wig that did not blend at all well with the greying hair beneath. He had a nose that reminded me of Charles Laughton's Quasimodo in *The Hunchback of Notre Dame*. And his nostrils pointed skywards like a double-barrelled gun.

He was in the backroom. We disturbed him while he was planing the lid of a coffin which rested on a carpenter's bench.

' 'Tis a sad day for the Dismal Trade when there is no funeral, Bottesford,' said Fr Duddleswell.

The undertaker went on shuffling his plane back and forth. 'People don't die to please me,' he snapped.

Fr Duddleswell asked to be taken to the Chapel of Rest in order to pray over Mr Dodson. Mr Bottesford's attitude changed at once from defiance to anxiety. He insisted he would have to go first and prepare the Chapel. It would only

take a few minutes and in the meantime he invited us to
take a seat.

When he went out, Fr Duddleswell seemed intent on taking something else. There was a large cabinet in the room
full of small drawers. Fr Duddleswell opened up one after
another until he came across the thing he was looking for.
Whatever it was, he put it smartly in his pocket.

He made a gesture towards the coffin nearing completion.
'Look at the quality of that wood, Father Neil. Orange
boxes banged together, nothing more. 'Twould not keep a
corpse dry in an April shower. Not only does he fake his hair
by putting a bird's nest upon his head, he also fakes coffins.
What can you expect, Father Neil, of a man who makes a
living out of death?'

Mr Bottesford returned puffing and blowing. He led us
out and across a small grey courtyard into his Chapel of Rest.
It wasn't much more than a large garden shed. Black drapes
from the war years kept out the light. In the centre was a
catafalque on which rested a superb oak coffin lit up at each
corner by candles of yellow-ochre. No orange box in this
case, I thought.

Fr Duddleswell suggested we all kneel for the *De Pro-
fundis*. '*Out of the depths have I cried to Thee, O Lord,*' he
began, '*Lord, hear my voice,*' and Mr Bottesford and I joined
forces with '*Let Thine ear be attentive to the voice of my
supplication.*'

When the prayer was over, Fr Duddleswell approached the
catafalque. 'I congratulate you, Bottesford,' he whispered, 'a
most beautiful coffin.'

'Casket,' Mr Bottesford corrected him with the term
favoured by the trade.

Without warning, Fr Duddleswell hammered on the coffin
lid with his fist. The effect in that confined space and waver-

ing light was shattering. Mr Bottesford and I almost embraced each other in fright. Fr Duddleswell repeated his onslaught on the coffin from various angles. His recent preoccupation with death must have unhinged the old boy.

'Bottesford,' he said threateningly, ''tis as hollow as is your heart. Where is he, tell me, now, this instant.' Had the undertaker sold the body for the purposes of necromancy or scientific research? Mr Bottesford pointed to an object in shadow by the wall. 'Bring a candle, Bottesford.'

The undertaker pulled one of the huge candles out of its socket and carried it with quivering hand to where Fr Duddleswell was standing. 'Take it off,' he ordered, pointing to a tarpaulin covering something of indistinct shape.

I turned away almost expecting to see under it Jack Dodson's corpse. It was only a second coffin. It had on it a brass plate with Jack's name, his dates of birth and death, and *R.I.P.*

'An orange box,' said Fr Duddleswell disgustedly, 'masquerading as a coffin.' Even by candlelight I could see that the coffin was neatly covered by a kind of wallpaper of oak design. Tear-filled eyes at a funeral might not notice it.

I was sickened by the undertaker's deceit, but worse was to come. Fr Duddleswell said imperiously, 'Take it off, Bottesford. The lid, unscrew it, Bottesford.' No doubting his meaning this time.

'I can't,' he said hoarsely.

'There is no need for an exhumation order, Bottesford. He is not buried yet.'

Mr Bottesford's nerves were completely out of control. He bowed his head and the crackling candle flame shot up and singed his hair. Sparks flew and there was the odour of acrid fumes. He dropped the candle, tugged his wig off and stamped on it.

Fr Duddleswell said, ' 'Tis but a foretaste of the cremation that the Lord has in store for you, Bottesford, if you do not alter the evil of your doings.'

I couldn't help feeling sorry for him as he stood there in the macabre light, bald and trembling. But Fr Duddleswell was still not content. ' 'Tis not there is it, Bottesford?'

'He's in there all right, Father, I swear it. Please don't make me unscrew the lid.'

'You know well enough, man, I said not *he* but *it* is not in there.'

'I don't know what the hell you're spouting about,' yelled Mr Bottesford, his spirit returning as he stooped to pick up his wig.

Fr Duddleswell put his hand in his pocket and pulled out a small object that gleamed in the candlelight. 'The ring, Bottesford,' he said, almost touching the undertaker's nose with it.

'You pinched it,' whimpered Mr Bottesford, lifting his head like a dog.

'No, Bottesford, you are the miscreant who pinched it. Black you are without and black within. Father Neil is me witness that I found this ring inscribed TO ME DARLING JACK in a drawer of your workroom. 'Twas not, I take it, the corpse that placed it there.'

He made Bottesford promise on his 'Catholic's honour' that the body would be transferred to the oak coffin—'casket', muttered Mr Bottesford, his professionalism coming through—and the ring replaced on the finger.

We returned to the workshop. 'Does the name Pinky Weston mean anything to you, Bottesford?'

It was evident to Fr Duddleswell that only the undertaker could have tipped off the Rapper because no notice of Jack Dodson's death had been posted on the church door. He warned Bottesford that if Pinky Weston had swindled old Mary, he would get the bill. A final admonition: 'Mend your devious ways, Bottesford, else I will see to it you no more box or heap the cold sod on parishioners of mine.'

On the way home, I expressed disgust at Bottesford's goings-on. Fr Duddleswell, firm in his charitable resolve, did not entirely agree. ' 'Tis true that grave-digger would con-diddle the chocolate out of a child's mouth.' All the same, Bottesford performed the least loved of the corporal works of mercy, bedding down the dead.

'A man's profession is bound to set its mark on him, Father Neil, if you're still with me. 'Tis no laughing matter tailor-ing wooden suits and attending a hundred funerals a year. For that he needs a heart that cannot feel and a nose that cannot smell.'

I reminded him of his words about Mr Bottesford making a living out of death. 'And do not we with our Requiems, lad? After all, Bottesford is not Adam. He did not invent death. Indeed, by raising the cost of dying, he might even be said to discourage it.'

Even when I mentioned the ring, Fr Duddleswell inclined to forgiveness. ' 'Tis easy to get hot under the round collar, Father Neil, but casting prejudice aside, to rob a cold ruin is not nearly so bad as robbing the living.'

I was thoroughly irritated by his willingness to excuse the undertaker. 'He robbed the living, too,' I said. 'He over-charged Mrs Dodson for the coffin.'

'Casket,' he corrected me with a wink.

'And nearly lost her that lovely silver pot.'

Overcharging Mary, he agreed, was a different matter. No recently bereaved person likes haggling over the price of a funeral. It seems mean and a slur on the memory of the departed. 'But then, Father Neil,' he said smiling, 'if I do not judge him too harshly for that even, d'you not think I owe him something?'

We were at tea when the doorbell rang. Mrs Pring announced that it was Mrs Dodson. In a flash, Fr Duddleswell was on his feet to invite her in. He paid no heed to her protests. 'Fetch Mary a cup, will you not, Mrs Pring? And, Mary dear, pity your poor feet and sit yourself down.'

Mary's story was that Mr Weston had prevailed on her to part with her Elizabethan pot for £75 in crisp new fivers.

'That's daylight robbery,' I cried.

Fr Duddleswell told me to hear Mary out and not get so uppity for God Almighty's sake.

Mary looked crestfallen at my remark. 'It's not as if my Jack had strong attachments to that pot, Fathers.' She went on to praise Mr Weston's honesty. He had accidentally twisted one of the handles and didn't reduce his offer for all that.

Fr Duddleswell flashed at me a warning to itch where I could scratch. 'Anyone in your position obviously has need of the money, Mary.'

Mrs Dodson explained that Jack's illness took up so much of their savings 'and we're—I'm—only an old age pensioner.' When the soil had settled on the grave she would now be able to afford a nice headstone.

Mary brightened up when Fr Duddleswell congratulated her on acting so wisely. All things considered, it was not a bad price. The pot *was* damaged. Pinky had to pass it on to a dealer who would want his rake-off, and selling to dealers is not always easy. Fashions change. Pinky took a risk in that there might not be a ready market for that kind of pot at this time.

'And now, Mary,' Fr Duddleswell concluded, 'tomorrow

we will lay your darling man to rest. No more thistles where he lies, Mary, and prayers of yours will provide him with pillows of roses for his head. Ah,' he sighed, ' 'tis nice to contemplate that when yourself gets to Heaven 'twill be a country where you are well acquainted.'

He took twenty-five pounds out of his wallet saying, ' 'Tis your lucky day, Mary. Only Saturday last I rid meself of a perfectly useless chair and would you believe it, now? this is what I was paid for it.' He thrust the money into Mary's hand before she could say no. ' 'Tis not for you, Mary, mind, 'tis for Jack. Towards his headstone, you follow?'

He led the widow to the door as if she were a queen. 'Make sure, Mary, you order him a *beautiful* stone.'

When he came back half singing, '*As leaves of the trees, such is the life of man,*' I tackled him with, 'Father, don't try and excuse Mr Weston's rotten trick this time.'

'Me soul detests it, Father Neil,' he replied earnestly. 'Would that I could poke me digit in his eye.'

'Imagine cheating a dear old lady out of so much money.'

'Abso-bloody-lutely, Father Neil, except that the pot was but a common or garden tea caddy worth less than half a dollar.'

Five

HELL AND HIGH WATER

'It's a lonesome wash that there's not a man's shirt in,' said Mrs Pring. My bedroom door was open and I could see her putting my clean linen in a drawer. I nodded, knowing that she was referring to the widow Dodson who had just gone home.

I offered her the opportunity for a chat. 'Going to stoke up my fire, Mrs P?'

A couple of minutes later she was piling on the coals in my study. 'At first when you're widowed,' she puffed, as she knelt at the fireplace, 'you can't believe it's true, or if it's true it can't be happening to you. It must be either a dream or someone in the War Office got the name and number wrong. Grief draws slowly like the morning fire.'

She talked unemotionally about losing her husband. It was a long time ago. A whirlwind war time courtship. Love at first sight and she never wanted another.

One thing bothered her: she could not honestly remember the colour of his eyes. 'I know they were a sort of greeny brown, Father Neil, but I can't picture them, you see?' I pursed my lips and nodded.

'We were only married a couple of months,' she went on, brushing the grate. 'My Ted was much younger than you, of course.' I was glad she did not see my reaction to that. 'I wrote to him straight away, soon as I knew, telling him that a little someone was on the way. But the letter came back with a batch of others, and with his effects. The only one unopened, it was. He was already gone, you . . .' She was still for a moment. 'Two months after, the war was over. All the killing stopped.' She paused again. 'Thank God.' I wanted to touch her on the shoulder but I was too shy. 'It meant my Helen was half orphaned before she saw the light of a candle.' She wiped her eyes on her sleeve because her hands had coal dust on them. As she got up, she said, 'I think people round here like talking to you, Father Neil.' I blushed at the compliment. 'You're a listening man.'

The change of topic was abrupt. 'At least *his* attack of the sullens'—she pointed below—'is over and he's back to abnormality.'

I sat her down and told her how Fr Duddleswell had tricked Pinky Weston. I expected her to show some disapproval but as usual when we were alone she was not too hard on him.

'He's as slippery as an eel's tail,' she said, 'but he never lied to the Rapper, did he, now? He only let him lie to himself.' She blew a stray hair out of her eyes. 'Ah, if only he was half as wicked as he thinks he is he'd be such a nice man. And much more fun to live with.'

Through the floorboards, confirming Mrs Pring's view that Fr Duddleswell's November blues were over, came strains of '*The flowers that bloom in the Spring, tra la.*' Perhaps it was this song that caused Mrs Pring's *lapsus linguae*. She said, 'He may be an old sour puss outside but never mind him, inside he's full of the springs of joy.' The song ceased suddenly when the telephone rang and Fr Duddleswell took the call.

Mrs Pring was keen to know if I felt really settled in St Jude's. In my reply I carefully avoided the word 'settled'. I said life was full of interest.

'Don't take too much notice of Fr D,' she advised. As his steps sounded on the stairs, she stood up. 'As you've probably guessed by now, his great weakness is the strength of his convictions.'

There was a thump on the door. 'Are you alone, Father Neil?' When I called out that only Mrs Pring was with me he made as if to retrace his steps saying, 'That giddy woman is too many for me altogether.'

Mrs Pring opened the door and signalled to him that she was on the point of leaving. She was not offensive to him, may be to reward him for his good work on behalf of widows.

His own uncharity and deviousness had returned full blast. 'I cannot understand why you associate with her, Father Neil,' he barked. 'In every other particular you are a commendable curate. D'you not know that herself would build a nest in your ear and twitter-twitter all the day long?'

'She was talking about her husband,' I said.

That quietened him down. ' 'Tis always the young,' he said, biting his lip, 'who die in old men's wars.' He settled into an armchair clutching a large tome. 'As to the purpose of me visit.'

First came a reminder of the next day's Clergy Conference on Life After Death. Interdenominational, it was to be held at St Luke's under the chairmanship of the Anglican incumbent, the Rev. Percival Probble. In addition to the three Anglican ministers, two Methodists and a Jewish Rabbi had agreed to take part. The true Church was to be represented by the two of us and Canon Mahoney, D.D. The Canon was Bishop O'Reilly's personal theologian. He had been deputed to keep us on the path of orthodoxy and answer all non-Catholic objections.

Fr Duddleswell handed me his tome. *The Mysteries of*

Christianity by Matthias Scheeben, priced $7.50. 'Hot from the States,' he said. The author was the greatest nineteenth century German theologian. 'I want you to mug up the passages on life after death, you follow? in case the Canon and meself are unable to cope, like.' He was being funny, I think. 'If the Protestants suggest we pray for reunion, we will do no such thing, you hear me? We are far too divided to pray with them for *that*.'

The phone call had been from Mother Stephen, Superior of the Convent. She had invited herself and Sister Perpetua, our sacristan, to the presbytery in thirty minutes time. No reason had been given for the visit but Fr Duddleswell needed no telling. It was the same every year. Mother Stephen wanted to cancel the Fireworks Display at the last moment. The pretext was usually the likelihood of damage to the Convent's lawn or trees, or complaints from neighbours about the noise, or the good sisters having to keep the children in order when they should be reciting the divine office in chapel according to the rules of their holy Founder. 'Be ready to buttress me should I begin to flag,' he concluded.

On the dot of five, *Laudetur Jesus Christus* from Mother Stephen and *Semper laudetur*, 'May Christ be always praised' from Fr Duddleswell. The Superior dismissed the offer of tea with a twitch of her bony hand.

'Fr Duddleswell, I have not come to ask you to cancel the Fireworks Display tomorrow evening.' So the old man was mistaken. 'No, Father, I have been obliged to cancel it myself already.'

Fr Duddleswell enquired the reason. He was unruffled as if he were used to setbacks of this sort.

'Two-fold, Father.' For first-fold, Mother Stephen had recently read a book on the Gunpowder Plot written by a convert to Catholicism. His thesis was that Guy Fawkes Day was a Protestant ruse to blacken Holy Mother Church. Guy Fawkes's attempt to blow up the Houses of Parliament in 1605 had been made a pretext to persecute Roman Catholics ever since.

'I should imagine, Mother,' said Fr Duddleswell, 'that had he succeeded, the whole country would have been beholden to him.' The joke was lost on the black shroud seated opposite him.

Fr Duddleswell stated politely that the Bishop had appointed *him* defender of the faith in this area and he was perfectly satisfied with the theological propriety of burning a straw man on a bonfire. In fact, it was irrefutable proof of Catholicism, a proof not immediately evident to Mother Stephen or to me. Protestants ridicule Catholics, he said, for making use of images in their religion, and here are the Protestants availing themselves of Catholic methods of festivalizing. Before Mother Stephen could object he instanced the burning of heretics at *autos da fé*, apart from Catholic belief in the retributive fires of Hell and Purgatory.

It convinced me that Guy Fawkes Day was a sound Catholic investment. Fr Duddleswell looked across at me as if to say, one down and one to go.

Mother Stephen was already fumbling in the folds of her habit for her second argument. 'This leaflet, Father,' she said, 'has been sent us by the Council. The police have co-operated with the fire brigade and the local hospitals to provide statistics of accidents to minors during last Guy Fawkes night.' She read out figures. Five children under ten had burned their hands and sixteen under six had burned their legs, and so on. It was pretty grisly.

Fr Duddleswell pretended to see no significance in the figures whatsoever.

'Fr Duddleswell, I have taken the liberty of going through the parcel of lethals you despatched to our Convent. Crackers, rockets, smellies, smokies, catherine wheels—a whole arsenal of destruction.'

Fr Duddleswell forced her to grind to a halt as he unfolded a leaflet taken from his inside pocket. He pressed out the creases noisily. 'Police statistics, Mother, on the local children killed on the road in the last year, together with the number of accidents on the pedestrian crossings themselves.' He smiled pityingly. 'You are not proposing, Mother, that children should be forbidden to cross the roads?'

The Superior accused him of flippancy. Crossing the roads was a necessity, whereas she was about to prove that a Fireworks Display was not. He was already promising that he and I would set off the fireworks. 'The only persons, Mother, in any danger are meself and me curate.' He seemed confident that Mother Stephen would agree to the Display on such generous terms.

'Fr Duddleswell, you may set yourself alight or indulge in any other solitary pleasure on our Convent lawn that brings you satisfaction. Our children will not be there to see it.'

She was rising to her feet when Mrs Pring banged on the door and entered without an invitation. Fr Duddleswell was annoyed at being interrupted at this delicate stage in the negotiations.

Mrs Pring, clasping a copy of *The Universe*, was not in the least perturbed. 'Father, I only wanted to ask you something about the Display tomorrow evening.' His face fell to below zero. 'Are you using the Holy Father's blessing?'

Fr Duddleswell thawed instantly and met her enquiry with a quizzical smile.

'Last New Year's Eve,' she explained, 'the Pope blessed the fireworks and the children of Rome. A lovely prayer, as you remember, Father. Will you be using this'—she pointed to where the prayer was printed in capitals in the newspaper—'or the one in the Ritual?'

Fr Duddleswell assured her that of course he would be using the Holy Father's own blessing written specially for such occasions.

Mrs Pring departed to be followed soon by Mother Stephen. She had been faced with a straight choice: to obey God or Caesar. Sister Perpetua bowed out her defeated Superior before winking at us.

'Sister Perpetua,' croaked Mother Stephen without turning round, 'would you kindly regulate the movements of your eyelids in the manner of which our holy Foundress would have approved.'

Mrs Pring expressed delight that the poor little orphans would not be deprived of a rare chance to enjoy themselves and Fr Duddleswell took the opportunity to relate his favourite tale about statistics.

In the west of Ireland, 'in the dark days', a local deputation approached the English Chief Secretary, then visiting, with statistics proving that they needed finance for the railway so they could send their produce to market. Next day, another deputation arrived with another sheaf of statistics proving conclusively that they needed food subsidies because not so much as a sprig of parsley would grow on their land. Fr Duddleswell laughed merrily before putting on a very posh English accent. ' "Now, my good man," said the Chief Secretary to the leader of the second deputation, "yesterday's statistics prove the exact opposite of yours. How do you account for it?" "So be it, your Honour," says the leader of the second deputation, "but y'see, yesterday's statistics was compiled for an entirely different purpose." '

The rest of that evening I spent with Scheeben, reading about death, judgement, Heaven and Hell.

After breakfast, Fr Duddleswell drove off to an unknown destination. He was back well in time to transport Canon Mahoney and me to the Vicarage.

In a committee room, we drank coffee before grouping around the table. The three Anglicans wore cassocks with capes which we always held to be an affectation. Of the two Methodists, Sobb was bearded and Tinsey was clean shaven. At the end of the table opposite Mr Probble sat Rabbi Epstein. He wore a broad-brimmed black hat on the back of his head, a bushy beard and spectacles that covered the rest of his face. He was still in a frayed black satin overcoat and, for some undisclosed reason, he had another draped across his knees. He came from somewhere east of Dover.

The Rev. d'Arcy, the Senior Anglican curate, read a thirty-minute position paper on 'Life after Death in the Old and New Testaments'. It contained frequent references to *zoè aiònios* which at first I thought was a girl's name until it dawned on me that it was Greek for 'eternal life'. Mr d'Arcy had read Greats at Oxford and his classical learning put most of what he said beyond my reach.

The first comment was made by Rabbi Epstein. Very politely he objected to the use of the *Old* Testament. 'You must remimber well,' he said in his broken English, 'that for us it only is the Jewish Bibble. *You* call him old because you think your Bibble is newer. For us, the Jewish Bibble is always newest.'

The Rev. d'Arcy apologized profusely for his careless use of terms in the present company.

'Thank you,' said the Rabbi—his 'th' was pronounced like a 'z' in the Slavonic fashion. 'Now where Heaven is? I ask myself.' Nobody round the table was anxious to help him answer his question. 'Where God is, there Heaven is.' He tapped his outstretched fingers together as if applauding himself. 'Heaven has not a place,' he went on in a semi-mystical vein. 'God is, as we say in Talmud "*ha-Geburah*, The Might". He is the place where the world is. That is what we Jews think.'

Canon Mahoney scratched his bald head and exchanged a glance with Fr Duddleswell indicating that it is not easy looking for the invisible wee folk in the pitch dark.

'We Jews,' went on the Rabbi, his eyes so radiant it looked as if two lighted cigarettes had been sunk in the sockets, 'we Jews believe passionately in *gehenna*, the pit of the fire.' Fr Duddleswell nodded approval. 'Also *Gan Eden*, the Garden of the Bliss and the Delight.' The Canon and Fr Duddleswell both saw signs of hope in that. 'In the pit of the fire,' continued Rabbi Epstein, 'the naughty boys go.' I could see my two colleagues beginning to wonder what differences remained between ourselves and our Jewish brethren when the Rabbi said, 'What more certain could be than that Jesus in the Garden of Delight is? He was a good Jew. But,' he swung his head like a pendulum, 'some of his followers, aaaah.' That 'ah' went down his throat like the last of the bath-water, in a noisy vortex, down the drain. Well, this was a curate's egg. The rest was all bad. 'The *very* naughty boys sometimes spend a whole year in the pit of the fire before they enter the Paradise.'

Everyone at the table disapproved of that, and the Rabbi, not wishing to proselytize, said nothing after that except, 'We Jews believe there are no ghettoes in Heaven and no pogroms in Hell.'

The fat Rev. Pinkerton, puffing on his cigarette without ever removing it from his mouth, delivered his opinion on

Hell. The fire was a symbol, like the worm that never dies and the teeth that gnash on endlessly, like Christ's command to pluck out your eye rather than let it look on wickedness.

Canon Mahoney, sucking his dead pipe, launched the counter-attack, ably supported by Fr Duddleswell. The Church has taught for nigh on two thousand years the reality of the fires of Hell and the eternity of the roasting prepared for those who die unrepentant. In this the Church was simply reinforcing the teaching of our Blessed Lord who five times in the course of the Sermon on the Mount stressed the everlasting pains of the damned.

The Rev. Pinkerton stubbed out one cigarette and lit another before commenting caustically on the arbitrariness of the Catholic God. Why should He cut off one man's life immediately after mortal sin and another's immediately after he had repented of mortal sin?

Canon Mahoney handled that with ease. God in His divine foreknowledge sees how both of them *would* behave whatever opportunities for repentance He offered them.

I was very glad the Canon was in my team. But, objected Fatty, did we really think God was so cruel as to punish eternally an evil deed done in time? Fr Duddleswell drily asked the Rev. Pinkerton if *he* expected to be rewarded eternally for some good deed he might do in time.

'Okay,' wheezed Fatty, blowing out and filling the room with a pillar of cloud, 'tell me how parents can possibly be happy knowing that their children are burning for ever in Hell?'

'It is the very sweetness of divine justice,' replied Canon Mahoney, 'that will obliterate the pain, as will the vision of the beatific God.'

Mr Probble was becoming increasingly agitated as the temperature of the discussion rose. He was smiling and mur-

muring words about keeping the ecumenical spirit alive and abiding by the Great Commandment to love one another.

Mr Tinsy, an alto, demanded to know if, in Catholic dogma, children were eligible for Hell. Fr Duddleswell replied that naturally they were, provided they had reached the age of reason.

'Which is?' peeped Mr Tinsy.

'Seven or thereabouts,' answered Fr Duddleswell. Catching sight of Fatty almost swallowing his cigarette in a rage, he explained that Catholics respect the dignity of choice even among God's little ones.

Mr Tinsy remarked that 'sevens' were not even old enough to play with fireworks.

The bearded Mr Sobb asked how fire could burn bodies *and* souls, and burn them for ever without consuming them.

It was just the question I was hoping for. 'May I?' I began.

'Certainly not,' snapped Fr Duddleswell, turning to Canon Mahoney for the official answer to that conundrum.

'Let the lad say his piece, Charlie,' the Canon said kindly.

I opened my Scheeben at page 693 and read in a trembling voice:

'Hell fire differs from natural fire in this respect, that its flame is not the result of a natural, chemical process, but is sustained by divine power and therefore does not dissolve the body which it envelops, but precerves it forever in the comdition of burning agony.'

I don't know if that answered the Methodists' objections, it certainly silenced them. It even seemed to precipitate the end of the Conference. There was only small talk after that.

We Catholic clergy repaired to the Clinton Hotel. The consensus was that there was no value in such conferences and the Canon would report this to the Bishop. Jews were as incomprehensible as a woman's tantrums. The Protestants, especially 'that fat twerp', were so stubborn in their unbelief that there was little chance of converting them.

'You'd as soon convert a cock into a hen,' suggested Fr Duddleswell.

Canon Mahoney peered moodily into his empty wine glass, proffered it to me to replenish and sighed, 'They went into a skid 400 years ago at the Reformation, Charlie, and they've been facing the wrong way ever since.'

It was a matter of amazement to us that men of the cloth could doubt the everlasting flames when they were written large and clear in the Holy Book.

The Canon savoured the wine on his tongue and smoothed out a crease on his head. 'No reverence have they, Charlie, for the Undebatables.'

' 'Tis the ultimate proof, Seamus,' said Fr Duddleswell, downing his last drop of heavy wet, 'that only the Catholic Church has the authority to keep the harsh truths of the faith alive in their pristine purity.'

Mrs Pring accompanied us in the car to the Orphanage. It was a clear, crisp, windless evening lit by moon and stars.

The Convent lawn, between bare trees, formed a kind of amphitheatre. My shoes were crunching acorns as we approached a huge bonfire built in a clearing with a Guy on top not easily distinguishable against the sky. Mother Stephen, for all her hesitations, had done us proud.

A few feet from the bonfire was a crate of empty milk bottles for the rockets and there were large flat stones for the crackers and the Roman candles.

A bell had been rung on our arrival and the children were parading in noisy expectation behind a rope at the opposite end of the lawn.

Fr Duddleswell crossed to greet them and they cheered. A

group of them came up to me holding their right hands aloft and telling me their ages, $5\frac{1}{2}$, $6\frac{3}{4}$ and so on. A minute fellow in a dwarf's cap and Wellington boots trod on my toe to attract attention and crooked his finger to make me bend down. 'A secret, Father. You won't split?' I promised. 'I'm two and four quarters,' he whispered.

I patted him on the head. 'Congratulations.' He crooked his finger again. 'Yes, son?'

'Can I have sixpence?' he said.

As soon as the nuns were present I shone a torch on to Fr Duddleswell's paper to enable him to read the Holy Father's blessing. Two sisters brought forward the fireworks which had been stored in a tin tub. These, too, he blessed. While the children sang two verses of *Faith of our Fathers*, he and I carried the tub towards the bonfire.

Fr Duddleswell wanted to begin spectacularly with a rocket. He put one in a bottle, lit the blue paper and we retreated to a safe distance away. The rocket rose about two feet in the air and nose-dived into the fire. Groans and ironic applause from the children. Mother Stephen's voice could be heard above the din asking for more respect for 'our parish priest'.

He tried again. After using five or six matches, our parish priest could not so much as set the fuse alight. He bade me shine the torch on the fireworks. They were standing in at least eight inches of water. Sabotage.

Mother Stephen crunched her way solicitously across the grass. 'Having trouble, Fr Duddleswell?'

'A temporary inconvenience, Mother, nothing more.' He motioned to me to join him. We returned to the car, to groans and catcalls from the Lord's little darlings.

Fr Duddleswell opened the car boot. There was a box of fireworks even bigger than the first. 'Never underestimate the opposition, Father Neil. As innocent as doves we must be but as wise as serpents, besides.'

The children adored the display. 'Oohs' and 'ahs' and spontaneous applause from them with the sisters dancing around as excitedly as anyone. Fr Duddleswell and I stuffed our pockets with 'lethals' and ran here and there letting off rockets and jumping-crackers and the catherine wheels which we had pinned to the trunks of trees.

Mother Superior reappeared out of the gloom with two sisters who were carrying an enormous iron grid on which were laid vast quantities of potatoes already half baked. 'With the compliments of the Convent, Fathers,' she said.

We put the jacketed potatoes at the base of the bonfire and Fr Duddleswell waved to the children, held up a lighted match and applied it to the tinder. It flared up at once, illuminating the Guy who, I had to confess, looked very much like our parish priest. Black sacking did for a cassock. Its head was a kind of white soccer ball with spectacles inked on, and a few strands of a yellow mop were plastered over the top for hair.

Mother Stephen, who had remained in the vicinity, said above the crackle and splutter of the fire, 'The only authentic replica of *you*, Fr Duddleswell, at present in existence.' Fr Duddleswell went closer to the fire to examine the insult. 'I do agree with you, Father,' his underestimated adversary went on. 'There is something terribly Catholic about burning somebody in effigy.'

Fr Duddleswell had approached too close to the blaze. The heat must have ignited the fireworks on his person for he suffered the same fate as Mr Bottesford. Smoke and sparks flew out of his right cassock pocket and loud rumblings were heard.

Mother Stephen and I had the same thought. I snatched

the first box of fireworks out of the tub and we each took a
handle and threw the contents over Fr Duddleswell. The fire
on him was extinguished with a swish. He jumped up and
down, damp, frightened and miserable. The children roared
more delightedly than ever as he gave a good imitation of
the *Danse Macabre*, etched as he was against the red flames.

'Was I not branded like a steer, now, Father Neil?'

In spite of the early hour, Fr Duddleswell was in pyjamas
and dressing-gown in front of the fire. Mrs Pring had brought
us both a cup of cocoa. ' 'Tis a good job me foundations are
firm, like.' The same foundations were turned to the fire in
the grate but not as close as before. 'Next year, I have no
doubts, I will appear in Mother Stephen's statistics with the
under fives and under tens. Imagine, now, "One under sixty
with a burnt bum." '

I told him to have no regrets. Mother Stephen was so impressed with his performance she might demand a repeat
next year.

'Ah, me one consolation in me hour of need was having a
curate to stand by me come Hell or high water.'

As I sipped my cocoa, it burned my lip. 'Father,' I said,
referring back to the morning, 'do you really think God will
allow a son or daughter of His to burn in Hell for ever and
ever?'

'In some cases,' contributed Mrs Pring, indicating her boss,
'the Almighty has no other choice.'

'But, Father, do you really believe that Scheeben stuff I
read out at the Conference?' Fr Duddleswell puffed and blew
and touched his scorched thigh. I persisted: 'People,
ordinary people like you and me and Mrs Pring?'

Fr Duddleswell looked at me witheringly. 'Father Neil.' A
pause, a deep sigh and a new beginning. 'Father Neil, Holy

Mother Church bids us believe docilely in the reality of the eternal fires of Hell. Yet who but a raving lunatic would claim there is anybody there?'

Six

ONE SINNER WHO WILL NOT REPENT

In early September, Fr Duddleswell had shown me how to make the rounds of St Jude's Junior School. It began in the playground before morning lessons. He crouched down to play marbles with a group of children. He cheated outrageously, kicking the marble in the right direction if his hand had 'not dealt kindly' with him. He always won. Afterwards, he sold the losers their marbles back at a reduced rate and gave the proceeds to more needy children—'like Robin Hood, you follow?'

In each class it was the boy or girl who could answer three Catechism questions in the shortest time without hesitations who received a silver threepenny piece. The winner had to go to the front of the class and fix it on his upturned nose. Failure to keep it there until he was back at his place meant Fr Duddleswell confiscated it on the spot.

He was convinced of the value of *The Penny Catechism*. It had served the Church well since Victorian times. It contained in a brief and eloquent form the main tenets of the Catholic faith. The child may not grasp all its subtleties at once, but in the years ahead, with maturity, would come recognition and guidance. Remembrance was guaranteed by the sheer music of the words.

'*God made me to know Him*,' he recited for my benefit, '*to love Him and to serve Him in this world, and to be happy with Him for ever in the next.*' He dared me to suggest that Shakespeare himself ever penned more memorable lines than those.

I started with the best of intentions one Monday morning armed with two hundred assorted marbles from Fr Duddleswell's collection in a canvas bag. Unfortunately, I was no great shakes at marbles and worse still at cheating. I made little contact with the children because I lost every one of my marbles in the first twenty minutes.

In Class Five, the nines to tens, the form teacher was a charming, fair-haired Mrs Hughes. Her class knew their religion so well I could hardly make up my mind which of them could repeat the catechism fastest. Eventually I decided that a dark-haired girl in the back row had pipped the rest at the post. I signalled to her to come to the front for her reward. Mrs Hughes whispered to me, 'That's Esther, Father.'

'Esther,' I said, giving her a silver threepenny piece in her grubby little hand, 'I hope you will always know your faith as well as you do today. And may it stand you in good stead throughout your life.'

There was a stunned silence in the class. I thought the other children did not agree with my verdict or were jealous.

When Esther had returned to her place nodding to right and left—with her tongue out, I suspected—Mrs Hughes whispered again, 'Esther is Jewish, Father.'

Out of the corner of my mouth, I whispered back, 'Are there any other non-Catholics, Mrs Hughes?'

'Only one, Father.'

'Would you point to whoever it is?'

Mrs Hughes gently stabbed herself with her finger. 'I'm a Methodist,' she said.

During that Christmas term I grew to like Mrs Hughes' class best of all. They were disciplined and yet alive and full of fun. The top class became so surly and disagreeable they refused to answer any of my questions even for sixpence. Not wanting to see them caned for a lack of interest in the religion of love, I was reduced to asking Mr Bullimore, the form teacher, to get them to write out their questions and put them in a box to which I alone had the key. I promised the children anonymity. Some of the questions were obscene, some merely abusive. Most were illiterate.

One contribution read: 'If it's a *free* cuntry why do I have to go to school eh? *and* drink milk. call *that* a free cuntry eh?' Another provided me with a piece of unwanted domestic information: 'In our hous we call dad Mosis cos he gives us 10 comandments evry day befour brekfirst.' Another was a plain affirmation: 'I don't like going to school bicause there's nothing to do when you get there except learn lots of things I don't wanner know. Another thing if they put old Bully on the telly I would switch him off before he came on.'

Interestingly enough, only the obscene ones were signed. No doubt with someone else's name.

On the morning after Fr Duddleswell had been 'burnt in more than effigy', I entered Mrs Hughes' class hoping for a taste of sanity. The children were their usual enthusiastic selves. Before I could finish any of my November questions on death, judgement, Hell and Heaven, they were bouncing their bottoms on their benches with vibrating arms outstretched and calling 'Please, Father, please, Father.'

When I had adjudged Philip in the front row to be the winner, I asked them a few more unscripted questions. 'I don't suppose any boy or girl has ever been to a funeral?'

Philip, of course, had been to everything. 'Please, Father. I went to a terrific funeral once.'

'Really, Philip?'

'Yes, Father. I saw these four dead men carrying a big box.'

Johnny, a Jamaican lad, said in a loud drawl, 'Souls don't get buried, do they, Father?'

'No, Johnny,' I assured him, 'souls go straight home to God. We only bury bodies.'

Johnny looked shattered at that. 'What do they do with the heads, then?'

Up leapt Robert, his hand in the air. 'Last year our granny came and died with us, Father.' Before I could offer him my condolences, he added joyfully, 'But we made sure she was dead before they planted her.'

Lucy Mary had more melancholy tidings. 'When Suzy my rabbit died and went to Heaven, Father,' she murmured, 'she left her carrot behind.'

Even this news did not dampen the youngsters' spirits for long. Mark said, 'Please, Father, our grandma died and went to Heaven and everyone's pleased but not grandma.'

Frank, a fat boy in long trousers, turned the tables on me by asking, 'My gran said when she gets to Heaven she'll pray for us. What makes her so sure, Father?' I said I could not answer that because I didn't know his gran.

'You must know her, Father,' Frank insisted, 'she wears glasses and brown shoes.'

'Mrs Phipps, Father,' said Sean breathlessly, 'Mrs Phipps who lives next door is dead but Dad say there's nothing else wrong with her.'

I was about to tell him that many people die only of death but satisfied myself by assuring Sean his Dad would not have said what he did if it wasn't true.

Sean had an afterthought. 'She's moved now, Father.'

To stem the tide a bit, I asked them what happens to people when they die. 'In your own words, please, children.'

That was inviting trouble.

Patricia, who looked like a little barn owl, spoke up for the rest of the class. 'If their soul's white they go to Heaven, if it's black they go to Hell and if it's got measles they go to Purgatory till it clears up.'

I glanced at Mrs Hughes to enquire whether she was trying to undermine Catholic teaching on life after death. She shrugged her shoulders disclaiming any responsibility for these heterodox opinions.

That was when I glimpsed Jimmy Baxter sitting at his desk to my right with tears running down his cheeks. It struck me that Jimmy, one of the brightest in the class, had not contributed anything that morning.

Ken piped up from the back row next to Esther. 'When my grandpa went to Heaven, Father, he was very, very old so I don't s'ppose he'll last there long, will he?' I was too distracted by Jimmy's tears to reply to that, or to correct Judy who called out, 'Stupid! In Heaven everybody's made of stainless steel, aren't they, Father?'

'Please, Father,' shouted Dean, the terror of the class, 'when you go to Hell can you take your dog with you?'

'Certainly not,' I said, still looking at Jimmy Baxter out of the corner of my eye.

'Mine likes it in front of the fire, Father.'

Mrs Hughes called things to a halt by telling the children to get on with their sums. It gave me the chance to ask her what was the matter with Jimmy. She referred me to the Headmistress.

Miss Bumple, of uncertain age, had been teaching long before systematic training had been devised for teachers. She was an amiable eccentric. Somewhere in her long campaign, she had been decorated with a cauliflower ear, the only one

I had ever seen on a woman. She still wore an earring in it. Her mother had had her ears pierced when she was a baby and it wasn't like Miss Bumple 'to waste the holes'.

Her eyebrows were white but her short cut hair was dyed an unnatural black. Fr Duddleswell had briefed me on her vocabulary which consisted basically of permutations of the one word 'egregious'. 'Egregious' for Miss Bumple meant 'normal'. 'Highly egregious' meant 'entertaining'. 'Exceedingly egregious' meant 'very funny'. 'Excessively egregious' meant 'intolerable', 'beyond the joke'.

For all her strangeness, Miss Bumple, according to Fr Duddleswell, was entirely trustworthy. Whatever you said to her in confidence went in one of her ears and was corked by the other.

On this November 6th, the Head, dressed in her usual tweeds, was in her jumble sale of an office surrounded by cups and trophies that looked gold until closer inspection revealed them to be of tarnished silver.

Taking a big pull on her cheroot, she rose to greet me. 'Fr Boyd,' she exhaled all over me with gusto, '*delighted*.' When she spoke she tightened her cheek muscles and pursed her lips as if she were about to blow a trumpet. Her voice, with an East London edge to it, was both musical and compelling. She grabbed my hand and almost wrenched my arm out of its socket.

I told her I was worried about Jimmy Baxter. 'Dearie me,' she said, 'that is not exceedingly egregious.' Jimmy's grandfather, Mr Bingley, had been poorly for some time and now was proper poorly. Jimmy was very attached to him. Since his dad had died, Jimmy had been brought up by his grandfather.

When I offered to help, Miss Bumple surprised me by her insistence that I was no use in this instance. Jimmy was

simply frightened that because his grandfather did not believe in God and never went to Church he would go to Hell
when he died.

'If, Fr Boyd, you tell children there is a Hell and that unrepentant sinners go there,' trumpeted Miss Bumple, 'they
are bound to draw their own conclusions. Mr Bingley, you
see, is a lapsed Catholic. This makes the matter'—she loosed
a huge current of smoke—'excessively egregious'.

I returned to the presbytery in an unhappy frame of mind.
Mrs Pring informed me that 'the Rooster' was in the garage.
I found him lying on an old rug underneath his car. When
I hailed him, he slid out and eyed me from the ground. He
had on a Churchillian boiler-suit, his face and hands were
covered in oil.

Bingley, J.J., he told me, had once been a model Catholic.
His misfortune was at the age of twenty-five to marry a girl
who turned out to be a whore. She had walked out on him
after only three months in favour of a Russian sailor. After
ten years, J.J. had divorced her and married again outside
the Church. His second wife was a Catholic, too. It was the
great sorrow of her life that she was barred from the sacraments. J.J. took a more truculent line. He repudiated the
harshness of the Church's teaching, renounced his faith in
God and joined the ranks of the Friday meat-eaters. He even
became a paid-up member of the Communist Party.
Maureen, his wife, had insisted all the same in bringing up
the two girls as Catholics. The elder of the two, Janice, was
Jimmy's mother.

I remembered that Mr Bingley was a widower. 'Hadn't
that made a difference?'

'Only for the worse, Father Neil. I anointed Maureen
and buried her meself. J.J. would not attend her funeral. It
made him even more bitter to learn that now his woman was

taken from him he was free to return to the Church. He would *not*. If his wife was deprived of the sacraments throughout their marriage, so would he be till his dying day. And I believe he is unshaken in his resolve. He is one sinner who will not repent.'

When he saw my eagerness to help he let me go to the hospital with the warning not to be disappointed if I did not succeed. 'J.J. is as loggerheaded a fellow as you are ever likely to meet.'

Jimmy's mother was by her father's bed at the end of a long ward. From a distance I could see them chatting. Mrs Baxter was tucking in the bedclothes and patting the pillow. When she caught sight of me, I thought I saw both pleasure and apprehension on her face.

I introduced myself. Mr Bingley was high up in the bed with his long white hair trailing on the pillow. His skin was taut over his face as though it were covered with a white stocking. And he stared right through me.

It was an unnerving experience. Nothing I said made any impression on him. Not a smile or the blink of an eyelid. As far as he was concerned I did not exist.

I spoke to Mrs Baxter. 'Would you leave us for a few moments, please?' Mrs Baxter immediately rose up and went. I explained very simply to the old man why I had come. Not for his sake but for Jimmy's. I told him about my visit to the school and Jimmy's tears.

He could have been carved out of granite. After a couple of minutes, I gave up, murmured 'God bless you' and joined Mrs Baxter in the corridor. She was crying. She knew her father hadn't long left. Jimmy, she said, would never get over it if her father died without confessing his sins so he could go to Heaven with grandma.

With nurses passing to and fro nearby, I explained as best

I could that only God knows what goes on in a man's heart. Someone could receive the sacraments and still be a bad man. Another could refuse the sacraments and still be humble and acceptable to God like the publican in Jesus' lovely parable.

It consoled her a little. 'But how can I explain that to a nine-year-old, Father?' she asked. 'Jimmy keeps saying grandpa commits a mortal sin every Sunday and Holy day by not attending Mass and I say it's not a new mortal sin each time, Jimmy.' She looked up at me to enquire whether or not she was propounding heresy. 'It's not a lot of mortal sins, is it, Father?' I didn't reply. 'Isn't it just one? A big one, perhaps? But just one?' She pleaded with me for a merciful reply.

'Once is enough,' I said hedging. I followed it with the only answer that would fit the situation, slightly modified from *The Confessions Of St Augustine*. 'It's impossible for Mr Bingley to perish when his little grandson is crying for him.'

Mrs Baxter said, 'Father, even if God is good to my father and he goes to Heaven, you won't be able to bury him with mum, will you?' I was not sure what Fr Duddleswell would say to that. 'It hurts, Father, the thought that dad won't be buried by a priest and they'll be separated in death after all their years together here.'

'Why don't you put that to your father, Mrs Baxter?'

'I have. He says my mum is only dust and ashes now and there'll be no separation because after death there's nothing.'

Fortunately, the ward sister was in her office. She confided to me that Mr Bingley was not expected to last more than a day or two. He could go any time. The drugs were very effective in taking away the pain and occasional whiffs of oxygen perked him up but there wasn't any long term hope.

I reported on my visit to Fr Duddleswell. He was surprised to learn that the end was near. He slipped out of his boiler suit and went to clean up. After that, I expected him to race off to the hospital but he made no move. He went into the church to pray. After a quick lunch, he did not take his siesta but returned to the church and stayed there until tea time on his knees. After tea, he proclaimed that at last he was spiritually ready 'to have a go at J.J.'.

Jimmy was with his mother at Mr Bingley's bedside. We were hesitant about breaking up a family group that would soon be dissolved by a sterner hand. I could not help admiring the old fellow for the strength of his convictions.

Fr Duddleswell went into the ward and soon Jimmy and his mother kissed Mr Bingley and came to join me. From afar, we saw Fr Duddleswell earnestly talking to Mr Bingley who treated him as he had earlier treated me. I could feel mother and child next to me grow tense with disappointment at the total absence of response.

Then Fr Duddleswell bent over and whispered something in Mr Bingley's ear. From then on, it was like watching someone on the receiving end of one of Jesus' instant miracles. The patient immediately sat up and spoke. Fr Duddleswell listened intently and bent over him again, at which Mr Bingley became quite voluble. We couldn't make out what was being said but he and Fr Duddleswell were deep in conversation. Fr Duddleswell brought it to an end by raising his hand high above the patient's head and bringing it down so sharply that had it landed it might have despatched him aloft straight away. We relaxed. It was only the first part of a huge blessing.

The Baxters' tears turned into tears of joy. Fr Duddleswell returned like a conquering hero. Jimmy spoke in secret to his mother and she gave him a silver threepenny piece which Jimmy fixed on Fr Duddleswell's nose. He couldn't keep it there and when it fell to the floor Jimmy pocketed it.

'Well, now,' said Fr Duddleswell warmly, 'you can both be content, like. I have done everything for him in me power. You can safely leave the rest to the Almighty.'

Mrs Baxter wanted to know if her father could now be buried in her mother's grave. Fr Duddleswell told her to ask Jimmy, and Jimmy said of course he could because he was a Catholic again.

On the way home, Fr Duddleswell said buoyantly, '*Nil desperandum*, Father Neil, Never give up, like.'

His long vigil before the Blessed Sacrament had paid off. I confessed I thought there was no chance of the old chap repenting. I had never seen anyone so hardened against the grace of God.

Fr Duddleswell recalled a phrase from a curious French writer Charles Péguy, a Catholic who could not bring himself to believe in Hell. ' "The appalling strangeness of the mercy of God," Father Neil. An apt description of the case in question, would you not say?'

I said I presumed he would return later and clean up, so to speak, by giving Mr Bingley Extreme Unction, Viaticum and the Papal Blessing.

'To be perfectly honest with you, Father Neil, 'twas not entirely as it seemed.' What had caused Mr Bingley to sit up was Fr Duddleswell whispering in his ear, 'J.J., you have been a bloody fool all your life and you will be a bloody fool to the bitter end.'

I was astonished. God's mercy *must* be appallingly strange if abuse can bring a lost sheep back to the fold when kindness fails. 'What did he actually say to that, Father?'

'He cast dreadful aspersions on the honour of me mother,

Father Neil. Then 'twas'—my parish priest was blushing—'then 'twas I bent down again and ... I bit his ear, God forgive me.'

'But at what point did he *repent*, Father?'

'Did not St Peter, the Prince of the Apostles himself sever Malchus' ear completely with a sword in the Garden?'

I repeated my question.

'Did I ever say to you he repented, now? Did he not swear at me and I at him? And did he not threaten to do unspeakable things to me if I did not sling my hook? That was when I nearly brought me fist crashing down on his head. Only the appalling strangeness of God's mercy sweetened me fury and transformed me blow into a benediction.'

'That was all?'

'Almost, Father Neil. His last solemn words uttered in me hearing were "Sod off." And that, me dear boy, is a euphemism, like.'

Fr Duddleswell and I were chatting about finance in his study next morning at ten when Mrs Pring ushered in Mrs Baxter. Her eyes were shining with joy and grief.

'He passed over in the night, Fathers.'

We signed ourselves. Fr Duddleswell said, 'May he rest in peace,' and squeezed her arm.

Mrs Baxter expressed relief and gratitude that at least her father had made his peace with God. She had already telephoned the undertaker and Jimmy had rushed off to school to tell Mrs Hughes the good news.

As she was leaving, Mrs Baxter said, 'It's a real case of between the stirrup and the ground, isn't it, Fathers?'

Fr Duddleswell kissed her hand. 'God's mercy, Janice, is fathomless.' She slipped him a five pound note for a Requiem Mass. 'Heaven be in your road,' he said.

Afterwards, he held the fiver up. 'Father Neil, it pays to be kind to the dying, does it not?'

I was more concerned to know how a professed atheist and card-carrying Communist was eligible for a Catholic burial.

He winked at me like a schoolboy. 'Father Neil, did I not tell you before that to please a child I would, in full regalia, bury a hedgehog or a tin mouse. I have no quarrel with the dead.'

When I tried reasoning theologically, he stopped me. 'That Rabbi at the Conference had something, Father Neil. No ghettoes in Heaven, no pogroms in Hell. Somehow I feel that in the Hereafter we shall all of us be model Catholics.'

He walked over to the crucifix on the wall and gazed up at it as though he were St Francis expecting the Crucified to talk to him. 'Tell me truly, now, Father Neil, was I right or wrong?'

I'm not God. I couldn't settle the matter of his conscience for him.

'The way I look at it, Father Neil, is this. Old J.J. made his daughter and grandson sad enough while he was alive without adding to their misery after he is dead.' Reflecting on Jimmy's tears I savoured the truth of that. 'J.J.,' went on Fr Duddleswell, 'was a kind enough man, kinder than was life to him, you follow? Deep in his heart, at a level neither you nor I could hope to reach, he was ever a Catholic and the dear Lord grasped him there with kindness.'

I said plainly that I agreed with him.

He flared up in anger at that. 'You have no business agreeing with me, you young whipper-snapper. I came to me uncanonical views only after years of blood, sweat, toil and tears. You are not entitled to such views until you have suffered likewise. *Agree* with me, indeed!'

I waited till he had simmered down. He picked up the five pound note again. 'D'you know what, Father Neil? Whatever malignities he uttered against me mother, I am going to send J.J. the most expensive wreath in the shop. Whether he likes it or not.' He smiled his dolphin smile. 'After all, 'tis not every day I lay to rest a corpse with me teeth marks on his ear.'

Seven

MY FIRST MIRACLE

Fr Duddleswell, having convinced himself that I was now settled at St Jude's and was keen to do hospital work, announced his intention of appointing me official chaplain at the Kenworthy General. I had stepped in for him on his days off but it was a sign of his growing confidence in me that I was to have full responsibility for 400 beds.

' 'Twill be an entertaining experience for you,' he promised. 'You will be surprised how the wickedest folk will be calling out for you immediately God horizontalizes them.'

His advice was very practical. I had to register in the Chaplain's Office the chief details about the Catholics, especially whether the patient was married or not. 'Mind you, Father Neil, I counsel you not to put that question to the women in maternity.' In his experience, it was often less embarrassing to ask them for the name and address of their next of kin.

He repeated the prohibition on lighting candles when baptizing an infant in an oxygen tent, otherwise a premature death would follow hard on a premature birth. 'The poor mother, you see, might not take too kindly to the speed with which her baby went to God. Another thing,' he said with a twinkle in his eye, 'do not bite too many ears, like.'

His main concern was my relationship to the Matron, Miss Norah Bottomly. 'An extremely funny woman, Father Neil.'

'A great sense of humour?'

'None at all. Nevertheless she is in every sense the biggest thing in the K.G. Like the mercy of God itself, pressed down and running over. Not that she has much in there,' he said, tapping his temple. 'There is less to her than meets the eye, that's for sure. Finally, let me warn you, Father Neil, that Matron is a model of rectitude, the sort that puts a premium on wrongitude.'

Matron was in her high ceilinged office on the ground floor. Not a pen or piece of paper or stick of furniture was out of place, MISS NORAH BOTTOMLY—that was the name on the door —looked as though she had been laundered and starched inside her dark blue uniform.

Her hand was as smooth and hard as a statue's. 'Be seated, please, Fr Boyd.'

Matron's sentences mostly began with 'We in the Kenworthy General' or 'Our policy is.' It was like being addressed personally by a Papal Encyclical. Every nook and cranny of the Hospital was, as it were, a valley in Wales. In a most chilling voice, Matron said, 'You will find a warm welcome in every ward, Fr Boyd.'

Perched on the edge of my chair, I kept nodding at appropriate moments with 'Thank you, Matron. Thank you. Thank you very much.'

Every word and gesture of this formidable lady was intended to impress on me that, in whatever Church I had been ordained, in the Kenworthy General she was High Priestess.

'In conclusion, Fr Boyd, may I be permitted to say this? For as long as you remain strictly within the province of caring for souls, there will be between us nothing but the most unbounded harmony, co-operation and good will. Now you may go.'

I scooped myself up and bowed and scraped my way to the door.

From the first I enjoyed my work at the K.G. As Fr Duddleswell had forecast, Catholics who had lapsed from the Church for twenty years and more were keen to see me. This may have been due to the strangeness and boredom of hospital life, or the sense of being nearer to God the nearer they were to surgery.

Twice a week, I chatted with the patients individually, heard their confessions behind curtains that could not be relied on to keep out the draught and, in the early mornings, took them Holy Communion.

In Prince Albert Ward, a man's ward on the third floor, I came across Nurse Owen. I had met her before on my occasional visits and I had seen more of her at the Bathing Beauty Contest in the summer. I was pleased that she was a Catholic. I instantly felt there was a very spiritual and loving atmosphere in Prince Albert Ward.

Lying in the second bed on the left was an African. I asked Nurse Owen if he was a Catholic because from childhood I had heard stories of white missionaries baptizing black people from morning till night until their arms ached.

Mr Bwani was not 'one of us' but a Muslim from the Gold Coast. Something drew me to Mr Bwani, may be my pity for him being a Muslim. I knew little about Islam beyond its ambivalent attitude towards the flesh. It forbade the eating of pork not only on Fridays as in Catholicism but throughout life, while it permitted polygamy. I was pleased if puzzled that Muslims are reputed to have a tender devotion to the Virgin Mary.

I stuck my right hand in my jacket pocket and blessed Mr Bwani from afar, praying for his welfare, bodily and spiritual. I don't know if it helped him any but I was aware of two big eyes peeping over the sheets like a bunker and following me along the line of beds. My impression was that he needed me.

On my second visit I was introduced to the Sister in charge of Prince Albert Ward. Sister Dunne was as spectacularly thin as Matron was robust. Even the staff called her Old Barbed Wire.

I also spoke to Dr Spinks. He had nodded to me before, this time he was keen to deepen our acquaintance. Winking at me, he drew me into Sister's office and closed the door. 'It's okay,' he said, 'Old Barbed Wire won't be on duty for another hour. Spinks is the name, Jeremy Spinks. Senior House Officer.' He rubbed his right hand down his white coat as if to rid himself of microbes before seizing mine. I took an instant dislike to him.

'I'm Fr Boyd.' I was already beginning to feel exposed without my title. 'Fr Duddleswell's assistant.'

Dr Spinks, in his late twenties, tough looking, tanned and with a close-cropped head, went into an eulogy on Fr Duddleswell. Talk about a super bloke. Talk about his reputation with the locals who still remember him fire-watching every night of the Blitz. Talk about the guts of the guy, risking his life time after time to rescue families trapped in blazing buildings.

I had to admit this was the first I had heard of it.

Dr Spinks was sitting on Sister's desk, his legs dangling below his white coat. For some reason he was trying to intimidate me and doing rather well. He suddenly turned on me. To get straight to the point, there was something I could do to help. 'Fr Boyd, we have an African patient on our hands.'

'Mr Bwani?'

'Come on board, Father,' he said urgently. 'I need your help to cure him.'

I felt a wild surge of apprehension. 'I'd like to, Doctor, but I know very little about medicine. You see, we barely touched on it in our moral theology when I was a student.'

Dr Spinks swivelled off the desk and stood over me. 'It's a problem of the mind.'

I really hate people who glue you with their eyes. 'I'm not very good at psychology either,' I rushed to say 'especially black people's psychology.' I thought I had better come clean. 'To be frank, I've never actually spoken to a black man.'

Dr Spinks tried soothing me. It wasn't exactly formal psychology I was needed for. A bit of horse-sense would be enough.

'What's the matter with him, Doctor?'

'He's dying.'

'Poor man,' I gasped. 'What of?'

'Nothing.'

I stood up to make him understand I thought he was having me on. He pressed me down, gently but firmly, until my pants touched the chair. 'It's no leg pull, please believe me, Fr Boyd. Mr Bwani is not a dedicated Muslim. He is riddled with superstition. And he's dying because he is utterly convinced that he's going to die.'

Mr Bwani was a member of a Gold Coast community which had settled in Colborne, West London. They had brought their own witch-doctor with them. This medicine man was hired to put spells on his compatriots. If a chap wanted a house or a bicycle or someone else's wife, he called him in, paid a fee and the witch-doctor went to work.

When I had heard Dr Spinks out, I expressed myself sceptical of such superstitions but he was adamant. When in the

Navy, he told me, he had come across someone in sick bay who was stoned out of his mind because a witch-doctor had put a spell on him. 'In fact,' he said, 'two perfectly healthy patients of mine who'd been cursed actually ended up in Davy Jones's locker.' I had no idea of the effect of fear on people brought up in the bush.

'Now, Mr Bwani, Father. He's convinced that this witch-doctor has poisoned his blood. It's beginning to boil. When it has boiled long enough, he's going to die.' I continued sitting there listening to this nonsense because Dr Spinks gave me no choice. 'Unfortunately, Fr Boyd, when Bwani was admitted, the nurse took his blood pressure. Normal routine, you understand. But it was the worst thing she could have done in the circumstances. He felt the blood build up in his arm and, as he put it, he heard it bubbling.'

The Doctor moved away, confident no one could be a sceptic after that. 'Since then,' he said, 'Bwani hasn't stirred from his bed. He won't talk or touch his grub and he can't sleep. He's lost nearly twenty pounds in two weeks.'

'I'd like to help,' I said, preparing to make a quick getaway.

'Good,' he said. 'I knew you wouldn't let him down.'

I did not like his hectoring tone. 'I'll say the rosary for him.'

'That's not enough.'

I promise to offer Mass for Mr Bwani, privately, of course, because he was an infidel.

Dr Spinks impressed on me that I was required to help Bwani back to health, not pray for his conversion or cast devils out of him with the sign of the cross. But now that I was on my feet, I was less daunted. 'I'm sorry, Doctor,' I said, mindful of Matron's warning. 'I'm here to save souls not lives. That's *your* job.'

Dr Spinks went red in the face. Talk about a Good Samaritan. Talk about that good guy Duddleswell rushing into burning buildings. 'Think he felt guilty,' he threw at me, 'because he wasn't a fireman?' Talk about this crazy religion lark that stops you saving someone's life when only you can do it.

I challenged him to prove that only I was able to help Mr Bwani.

'Father,' he said, 'you must have seen those eyes following you up and down the ward. He looks on you as a white witch-doctor.'

I repudiated such a ridiculous title.

'I didn't say you *are* one,' he explained, 'only that he thinks you are. As far as he's concerned, you're the only one who might be powerful enough to break the spell he's under.' The whole matter, I felt, was now moving along humanistic lines. 'Father,' he said, 'I don't doubt that prayer works wonders in the long run but we're short of time. Bwani could be in the morgue in a couple of weeks.' His manner became menacing. 'You and I have got to use medicine.'

'No,' I said with alarm.

'Unorthodox medicine.'

'Doctor, I don't like unorthodox *anything*.'

In a final burst of exasperation, he asked, 'Father, are you going to help me or aren't you?'

I refused to be brow-beaten. 'May be,' I said.

Seeing he was making no headway, he invited me to the staff canteen. We bought ourselves coffee and joined Nurse Owen who was sitting alone drinking tea. If this was part of a prearranged plan I had no objections. After all, she was a Catholic.

Nurse Owen confirmed Dr Spinks' story. She felt personally responsible because she was the one who had taken Mr

Bwani's blood pressure when the trouble began. 'I could think of no more fitting role for a priest, Father,' she said, her eyelids fluttering attractively. 'Jesus was a priest, wasn't he? and He went all over Palestine healing the sick.'

Jesus Himself might have had second thoughts with someone like Miss Bottomly around. 'That's true,' I agreed.

Dr Spinks saw the opportunity to open out his plan. In every ward, next to the Sister's office, there was an amenity room usually reserved for the more serious cases. Bwani could be placed in there for observation. All I had to do was don my brightest Mass vestments and utter incantations over him. When I requested further elaboration, he mentioned incense, burnt feathers, chickens' blood and foreign-sounding formulas. It had to look authentic. He couldn't guarantee this would work but certainly nothing else would.

I had had a belly-full. I thanked him for the coffee and took my leave. I made one promise: I would mention the matter to Fr Duddleswell. That was safe enough. I already knew his enlightened views on superstitious and ungodly practices.

Fr Duddleswell heard me out with intense amusement. I was relieved to hear him deride Dr Spinks' proposals. I said, 'If Mr Bwani's going to die, Father, we'll have to accept it as God's will.'

'God's will, Father Neil?' he smiled. 'God's *will*? Let me tell you this, lad. If the will of God were done on earth as 'tis in Heaven 'twould lead to an impossible state of affairs.'

He was opposed to the Doctor's plan because he did not approve of voodoo and black magic, yet might there not be another less objectionable path to the same end? He left me in Limbo for twenty-four hours while he pondered. Then:

'Father Neil, is there any reason why you should not heal

this coloured gentleman with a perfectly straightforward miracle?'

I thought Fr Duddleswell's plan scarcely less bizarre than the Doctor's. Someone seeming to be seriously injured is to be planted in the amenity room alongside Mr Bwani. The nurse calls me in to cure him—not too difficult, seeing there is nothing wrong with him in the first place. Mr Bwani is so impressed, he is prepared to consider a cure in his own case.

I had a terrible vision of Miss Bottomly discovering my misdeeds. 'But, Father, remember the Matron,' I said apprehensively, 'I assume . . .'

He cut across me. 'Father Neil, you would be well advised to leave assumptions to the Blessed Virgin. Let me do the worrying, will you not? Was I not already several years a priest when you were still smoking your dummy?'

Certain aspects of his plan still puzzled me. 'What kind of serious injury did you have in mind?' I asked.

'Why not a compound fracture—say, a leg broken in a couple of places? The leg will look very fine when 'tis splinted and wrapped.'

I protested with my usual vigour. I was not going to lie by claiming a man's leg was broken if it wasn't.

Fr Duddleswell put on his offended air. 'I was suggesting no more, Father Neil, than that you should say the patient's leg bends congenitally in two places.' And seeing me still puzzled, 'At the knee and ankle, you follow?' I followed though I had no wish to. 'You simply enter the room, sprinkle your patient who has a . . . bent leg with holy water . . .'

'*Holy* water, Father?'

'Secular water, if you prefer, straight from the pump, and *Miracolo!* much to Mr Bwani's astonishment, his partner in misfortune takes up his bed and walks.'

'Who does, Father?'

'Your patient.'

'But who *is* my patient?'

'Father Neil, this is your miracle, is it not? You can surely
find some discreet parishioner to assist you in this charitable
enterprise? A quick change into pyjamas and he will soon be
restored to health, you can guarantee that.'

Fr Duddleswell asked for a few days grace to 'cogitate me
plan further, like'. In the meantime, I was to set about finding a candidate for a Lourdes-like miracle.

It was becoming clear to me that things were going to
have to get worse before they got even worse.

'Hello, Archie. Glad to find you at home.'

' 'Ello, Father.' Archie, my ex-crook friend, was pleased to
see me. 'Come up the apples and pears.' As we ascended the
stairs past the fat landlady who had let me in, Archie said,
'Got another job for me, then, 'ave yer, Father?'

I told him there was no one better qualified for what I had
in mind.

Archie shared a dingy, second-floor flat with the retired
accountant Peregrine Worsley. Peregrine was seated com-
fortably, his shirt sleeves rolled up, reading *The Sporting
Times*. He carefully folded his paper, removed his bi-focals
and rose to greet me. 'Delighted, sir, to make your acquaintance.' I reminded him that we had met only a few weeks
before when, for reasons of his own, he had told me of
Archie's criminal record. He said, 'Ah, yes, sir, but I meant
informally, out of hours, for a *tête à tête*.'

Now I knew Peregrine himself was not the irreproachable
citizen I had once taken him for. I liked him a lot.

'A pint of pig's ear, Father?' asked Archie.

'Not for me, thank you.' I explained at length the purpose of my visit.

'What a set up,' whistled Peregrine at the end of it.

'Cripes, what a con man you'd 'ave made, Father,' said Archie. I did not turn down the undeserved compliment. ' 'Course,' went on Archie, 'I wouldn't dream of lyin'.'

I said I honestly hadn't meant it to be a lie but that if he felt it was a problem ...

Archie cut in, 'No, 'taint no problem, Father. I did break one of me clothes pegs uncommon severe, not four years past.'

I was relieved that the way seemed clear for us to deceive Mr Bwani without any hint of a lie.

Archie had been making a dash from prison. He was just over a twenty-foot wall when the rope snapped 'and so did me bleedin' leg'.

After begging my pardon, he went on, 'I was laid up for six weeks with one leg in the air like a blinkin' can-can dancer.' Archie paused reflectively. 'Funny thin', Father. That's the only ever time I got remission for good conduct.'

Much to Archie's disgust, Peregrine wanted to talk terms. 'As to "the actual", young sir, how much remuneration will we be entitled to, should we manage to pull off this daring escapade?' I suggested a fiver. 'For each of us?' asked Peregrine. I nodded. 'Done,' concluded Peregrine, bringing down his paper on his knee like an auctioneer's hammer.

Archie coughed apologetically. 'Manners,' he said, putting his hand to his mouth. 'Am I s'pposed to wear pyjamas for this job, Father?'

'Only for a few minutes, Archie. I promise you there'll be no embarrassment.'

' 'Taint that I mind taking off me round the 'ouses in public, Father. But, straight up, I've not 'ad a pair of pyjamas since I was a kid in Borstal.'

Fr Duddleswell was developing his plan in ways that boded ill for my future. He came home one day bearing a number of boxes and jars with strange symbols on, and a book which he had borrowed from the Municipal Library. I was unfortunate enough to notice that it was entitled *Elementary Chemistry*.

He went immediately to his bedroom and locked himself in. For three days, he spent all his spare time there. From the cracks in the door emerged thick vapours, evil odours, the sound of bubbling and the occasional bang.

Before supper on Wednesday, Mrs Pring warned me that Fr D was sporting his antlers. He had obviously done something 'tragic to his few head whiskers'. He must have been trying to invent a lotion either to make them grow or to dye the grey hairs.

Fr Duddleswell came down to eat in his biretta. The hair below it was a bright green. Neither Mrs Pring nor I made any reference to it during a subdued meal. When it was over, he monopolized the bathroom till bedtime.

Next morning, he announced that he had made all the necessary arrangements with Dr Spinks on the telephone. Thursday, being Old Barbed Wire's day off, was D-Day. He communicated 'the further refinements of me plan' and it would have been ungenerous of me not to admit that they were brilliant. But I had lived with him long enough by this time to know that he always had more up his sleeve than his elbow. When I showed reluctance to go through with it without being party to all the facts, he reprimanded me sharply. 'Deep is the rumble of a bull in a strange pen', he said inconsequentially.

'Right, Father', I said, 'you win. I'll do it next week.'

'Next week, lad?' he said with scorn. 'Next *week*? You will be doing it the day before tomorrow.'

We walked under a dappled sky to the Kenworthy General. I was carrying a new pair of pyjamas in a paper bag. In the lobby we teamed up with Dr Spinks who had already introduced himself to Peregrine and Archie.

On the stroke of ten we sneaked into Sister Dunne's office. Nurse Owen, having seen to it that the walking patients were in the day-room, was in the amenity room fussing over Mr Bwani.

Archie, without a blink, changed into my best pyjamas. They were several sizes too big for him but he was like a boy scout donning his first uniform. 'Can I keep 'em after, Father?'

'Sure, Archie,' I whispered, hinting that he should keep his voice down.

Dr Spinks asked Archie to sit on a chair and he started to cut off the left leg of the pyjamas with scissors.

'Nark it, Doc,' moaned Archie, a pearl in each eye. ''Ave you got to do that?'

'Sorry, chum. When the bandages are removed, I want Mr Bwani to see *these*.' He traced with his finger where Archie's leg showed signs of a nasty accident. Archie acquiesced, then settled down on a trolley from the operating theatre while the Doctor splinted and bandaged his leg. 'Pity I can't put it in plaster,' he grinned, 'but this is the best I can do in the time.'

'It's only a game, Doc,' said Archie.

Dr Spinks was saying that on the contrary it was a matter of life and death when he saw that Archie was eyeing his colleague. Peregrine, standing aloof with his hat on and leaning on his rolled umbrella, began to phip-phip like a sparrow. He took off his bowler with a flourish and advanced with a wallet in his hand. 'Archie's quite right, Doctor. A child's prank.' Dr Spinks thrust the wallet into his back pocket without a word and went on bandaging.

'Father Neil,' muttered Fr Duddleswell, 'I commend you for your talent in casting such an *admirable* pair.'

At 10.15, Nurse Owen appeared and took charge of the trolley on which Archie was lying flat out. Peregrine, once more his serene self, put his bowler hat under his arm, adjusted his spectacles and prepared to accompany the bier. He touched Nurse Owen's shoulder, 'No tears, please, my dear.'

Fr Duddleswell said, 'You stay here, Father Neil, you are not required yet.'

Through the partition I could hear Peregrine and Archie talking in exaggerated tones as though rehearsing for a Christmas concert in Wormwood Scrubs. They were determined to earn their money.

'Does it hurt, Mr Lee?' I could just make out Nurse Owen's gentle voice.

'Doctor,' exclaimed Peregrine, 'has his leg been *broken?*' It was melodramatic but Mr Bwani, cowering under his blanket, might appreciate it.

Dr Spinks replied that a leg broken in two places, as was Mr Lee's, normally takes months to heal. With that, Doctor and Nurse joined me in Sister's office from where we heard Peregrine bidding adieu.

Archie said, 'I'm goin' to call in a real doctor.'

'A specialist, you mean?'

'A *real* doctor,' repeated Archie.

'Well, so long, old chappie,' drawled Peregrine. 'See you in a few months time if not before.'

He came into the office and whispered in my ear that in

his considered opinion his faultless performance entitled him to a tenner. When I refused, he went off in a huff. A few seconds later, a hand appeared round the door and stayed there palm upwards until I had put a fiver in it. It closed, turned over and waved goodbye with a wag of the index finger.

I heard Archie ask, 'Been in 'ere long, then, 'ave yer, mate? No audible response from Mr Bwani. Suddenly Archie burst out, 'Goo-er, me bleedin' leg. Just like that tea-leaf of a doctor to tie the bandages too tight. I'm losing all the circulation in me blood. " 'Ell, said the Duchess." ' Then more calmly: 'What's yer name, mate?'

Mr Bwani, perhaps out of compassion for the state of Archie's blood, must have mentioned his name. 'Bwani,' cried Archie. 'You're not Irish, I s'ppose. A joke, mate, no offence. Dunno about you but ever since I was a kid I've 'ad the mockers on me, grasp me meaning?'

'Yessir.'

'Nurse,' shouted Archie, 'I want my priest, do you 'ear?' Then more softly: 'Bwani boy, I've got a priest that'll shift me out of 'ere quicker'n you can say Man Friday. No 'arm meant, mate.'

'Yessir? Really, sir?' Mr Bwani was becoming garrulous.

When Archie went on to say I work miracles every morning before breakfast, it distressed me that, after a promising start, he should resort to telling lies.

'Yeah,' went on Archie. 'In church 'e conversations with Gawd and brings 'Im down to earth on a little stone. You b'lieve that, Bwani boy?' Archie was keeping strictly within the bounds of truth, after all.

'Nurse,' bawled Archie again, 'get me Fr Boyd.'

I took a deep breath and prepared to play the star role. Fr Duddleswell restrained me. 'No hurry,' he said. 'Give them another thirty minutes together. We do not want to break up a beautiful friendship, like.'

The interval was filled with Archie's virtual monologue in praise of his priest, punctuated by screams for the same to be sent to him at once. Finally, Nurse Owen led me in.

'Thank Gawd you've come, Father,' cried Archie.

Mr Bwani, his face glum as a pickled walnut, was half raised up on his pillow. That seemed a good omen but, on orders from Fr Duddleswell, I took no notice of him. 'What's up, Archie?' I asked.

'Me leg's been broke, Father, and me life's got the mulligrubs. You are Gawd's man, Father, so please 'elp me.'

I bade Archie put his trust in me, drew out my Roman Ritual and started reciting Latin prayers. I went through the baptismal ceremony and the blessing of a pregnant woman, followed by the thanksgiving for a safe delivery.

'Nurse,' I said, 'hand me the water.' I sprinkled Archie with it. Some spattered Mr Bwani who promptly dived under the sheet. I was relieved to see him reappear immediately. At all costs, he must not miss the next bit of the show.

'Nurse,' I ordered, 'remove this man's bandages. He is healed.'

I saw amazement in Mr Bwani's eyes. He lifted himself up to get a clearer view of Archie's hairy leg.

'Me smeller and snitch,' said Archie touching his nose, 'tells me I'm as good as new. Just the odd scar where the fractures was.'

'Stand up, Archie Lee,' I commanded.

He stood up, shakily because the bandages really had interfered with his circulation. It added conviction. 'I can walk again, Father,' Archie proclaimed ecstatically. He knelt down to kiss my feet. ''Ow can I ever thank yer enough, Father?'

I acted the real cad. 'By keeping the commandments, Archie, and by attending Mass on Sundays and Holy days. Will you promise me that, Archie?'

'Tell you what, Father,' said Archie, taken aback. 'I'll give it a lot of thought.'

The three of us left the amenity room. I judged it best not to speak to Mr Bwani. The first move would have to come from him.

Archie got dressed and I paid him his fiver. As he was leaving, he said, 'We're a smashing team, Father. Any time you wanner work another miracle, send for Archie.'

I gave him my word and watched him amble off with his precious pair of one-legged pyjamas tucked under his arm.

Nurse Owen returned to the amenity room to remake Archie's bed. I distinctly heard Mr Bwani say, 'Nurse, I want to see heem.'

'Who, Mr Bwani?'

'The prist. May I see heem? Pliz, Nurse.'

Fr Duddleswell rubbed his hands. ' 'Tis taking,' he said, 'but do not be too anxious to perform your miracles, Father Neil. Let us go home to lunch, and at 3 o'clock this afternoon he should be nice and ripe for a cure.'

'Hand Fr Boyd the syringe, Nurse.' Dr Spinks was about to rehearse in detail Fr Duddleswell's methods of healing Mr Bwani. 'You'll need first to draw out a drop of blood.'

I saw the vengeful gleam in his eye. 'Whose?' I asked.

'Before you take a blood sample from Bwani, Fr Boyd, you'll have to take one of your own.'

'Can't *you* do it, Doctor?'

'Afraid not, chum. It's vital that you draw out some of your own blood in Bwani's presence.'

'Father Neil,' put in Fr Duddleswell, 'will you please stop

141

moaning like a seal. Cannot you see that you have to obtain Mr Bwani's total confidence? You are the witch-doctor, not Dr Spinks nor anyone else. So take a sample and I will tell you what to do with it.' When I recoiled, he asked cruelly, 'Did not Jesus shed his blood for you?'

'No, Father,' I corrected him, 'other people shed it for him.'

Fr Duddleswell was in no mood for splitting hairs. 'Get on with it, now,' he threatened.

Nurse Owen tied a piece of rubber tubing round my upper arm; she rubbed the crook of my arm with a small disinfecting pad and said, 'Choose the biggest vein, Father.'

I asked if I could sit down. Nurse Owen brought me a chair and patted my shoulder. It gave me the strength I needed. I dug the needle in. She put a glass to my lips and I drank a few drops before raising the top of the syringe with my thumb and drawing up a fraction of blood. It was like being asked to operate on myself.

'A bit more', urged the prodigal Dr Spinks, 'you've lots to spare.' I drew out another half an inch and he was satisfied.

I extracted the needle. Nurse Owen swabbed the tiny puncture and wiped my brow with a cool, damp cloth. 'You're so brave, Father,' she said, and it seemed then all worthwhile.

Dr Spinks poured the remains of my glass into the saucer and added my blood to it, tinting the water. 'Right,' he said, 'action stations.'

I accompanied the Nurse to the amenity room. 'Now, Mr Bwani, I believe you wanted to see me.'

He indicated that he would like to whisper in my ear. He said, 'Mr Prist, sir, my witch-doctor curse me and I go dying.'

I nodded gravely. 'I believe you, Mr Bwani.'

His face lit up with joy at having found at last a healer

who did not ridicule his plight as so much jungle nonsense. 'Mr Prist, I want you pliz to uncurse me. My blood, she boil. Terrible hot already, Mr Prist, sir.'

'Powerful curse, Mr Bwani. Power-*ful*.'

'Yessir, yes-*sir*.'

The tray which Nurse Owen was carrying held a medicine glass, two saucers and a syringe. I gingerly fingered the syringe and took another sample of my blood from the identical hole. I emptied the contents on to the liquid in the first saucer and turned it red. 'Now, Mr Bwani,' I said, 'it's your turn.'

He eagerly stretched out his arm. He did not flinch as I dug the needle in but at the sight of his own blood rising in the syringe he shuddered violently.

I pressed out the contents on to the liquid in the second saucer. Even I was staggered at the way it started to froth and bubble and smoke. Hydrogen peroxide is potent and evil-smelling stuff.

Mr Bwani's eyes popped, his mouth gaped like a frog's and he fell back stiffly on his pillow. I thought he was dead and wondered how Matron would react to the news. Nurse Owen, unperturbed, raised Mr Bwani up and tried to coax him back to consciousness.

'Mr Bwani,' I said, slapping his face. At the fifth attempt, he heard me. 'Mr Bwani, heap plenty trouble here.'

'Plenny trouble,' he managed to gasp.

'Powerful medicine of black witch-doctor. Power-*ful*.' He attempted to voice his agreement but no words came. 'Me much more power-*ful*,' I said, continuing to give as good an imitation of a Red Indian chief as I could. 'Me put bigger spell still. You want?'

He wanted all right. Out came the Ritual and more Latin. I sprinkled him with water and made an impressive sign of the cross over him. Then I handed him the strong sedative in the medicine glass. As he relapsed into sleep I kept up the prayers, adding more promises to complete his recovery as soon as he came round. 'When you awake, Mr Bwani, no more hot blood. You be cured. No more curse.' My voice helped hypnotize him. 'Sleep, sleep, Mr Bwani.' He slept and snored mightily.

Dr Spinks had prepared about twenty ice-packs. We put them in the bed around Mr Bwani. Within twenty minutes his face whitened and his teeth started chattering. I was worried that he might get pneumonia or frostbite. The Doctor said this would help convince him that his blood had stopped boiling.

As he began to come to, we took away the ice-packs and brought in another tray. When everyone else had withdrawn, I patted Mr Bwani on the cheek. 'Awake, Mr Bwani, awake. Blood no boil no more.'

He kept repeating something like 'Bloody cold'. When I had interpreted it I said, 'Yes, Mr Bwani, blood cold, very cold.'

Soon he was restored to teeth-chattering consciousness. Once again, the trick with the syringe, his arm only. This time, his blood tinted the water without causing the slightest tremor on its surface.

Mr Bwani beamed. 'Curse fineeshed, Mr Prist. You are my father, my brother, my mother, my seester!'

Within a few days, Mr Bwani had put on weight and was completely well. Since he was to be discharged the following Thursday I was able to visit him undisturbed by Old Barbed Wire. I made him a present of a syringe and told him that should the witch-doctor curse him again he need not worry. My blessing was permanent like an injection against polio.

He would be able to prove it easily. 'Take saucer of water and put in drop of blood. Not too much, leave some in arm, savvy?'

Mr Bwani proclaimed, 'You are my father, my brother, my mother, my seester.'

These and many other relatives and friends, all gaily clad, were waiting for him in the vestibule. As soon as they saw him they broke into song. Mr Bwani made me anxious by telling the crowd that his recovery was due entirely to the white witch-doctor, at which they broke into loud applause.

When they left, I was about to go home myself when the fat Anglican curate from St Luke's, Mr Pinkerton, passed me puffing on a cigarette. 'There's a missive for you from Norah in the Chaplain's Office,' he said. 'I'll pray for you, old boy.'

This was the first note I had received from Matron. It was headed: REF: PRINCE ALBERT WARD and contained a brief injunction to appear before her that very day at 12 o'clock.

The next hour was spent in anguish and recriminations. The Bwani affair was bound to leak out, I was a fool not to realize that. Was it a criminal offence, I wondered, to practise medicine without qualifying as a doctor? Would Bishop O'Reilly haul me up and ask me to justify my extraordinary methods of evangelization?

I did not regret what I had done because I had saved a man's life. I regretted terribly what I had done for less elevated motives. One thing I was clear about: I would not implicate Nurse Owen in any way.

When I met Matron, she did not look any more severe than I had remembered her to be. 'It's about what happened in Prince Albert Ward, Fr Boyd.'

'I think I can explain, Matron,' I blurted out, not knowing what on earth I would say once I started.

'There is nothing to *explain*, Fr Boyd. This letter says it all.' She put on her pince-nez and addressed me over them as though I were a refractory audience. 'It is from a retired Chartered Accountant.'

Hell, I thought. So Peregrine has split on me just because I wouldn't pay him an extra five quid. Iscariot!

Matron read the letter. It stated in three or four tortuous sentences that Fr Boyd had proved himself a marvellous chaplain when his friend Archibald Lee had been a patient in Prince Albert Ward. He had not only helped Archibald spiritually but also financially when he was down on his luck. He begged Matron to thank Fr Boyd personally for his ministrations.

'Really, Matron,' I stammered with relief, 'there is no need ...'

'Indeed there is not, Fr Boyd,' whence she proceeded to lecture me in a booming voice on the fact that she had sternly warned me in our first encounter to restrict myself to the religious sphere.

I have never seen a bittern but she looked like one.

'What you do with your money outside these walls, Fr Boyd, is entirely your concern. But here in the Kenworthy General we leave financial matters to the Lady Almoner.' She stressed that this was the last instance of indiscipline she would tolerate in her Junior House Chaplain. I was dismissed.

It was Purgatory but I had been expecting Hell.

At the presbytery, Fr Duddleswell asked if I had seen the black man safely off the premises. I said yes.

'Ah,' he complained, 'when medical science was powerless you prevented him dying by utilizing all the resources of the faith and doubtless you did not receive so much as a Mass stipend.'

I confirmed that the miracle was free on the National

Health. I did not say I was worse off to the tune of ten pounds and a new pair of pyjamas. He was himself a witness to the fact that I had shed blood for the cause.

Fr Duddleswell screwed up his eyes. 'Did he ask to become a Catholic, like?'

'No.' I said.

'Imagine that, now, Father Neil. You pull him back from the edge of the grave and he remains an infidel.' For a few moments he pondered the inexpressible sadness of a priest's life. 'Bloody heavens, Father Neil,' he exploded at last, 'what will you have to do to make your own first convert – raise the dead?'

Eight

A THIEF IN THE PARISH

'As a seamstress, Father Neil, she is without equal.' Fr
Duddleswell was pointing proudly to the patch on his cassock
around a previously charred right pocket.

'Magnificent,' I said, surprised at this rare paean of praise
for Mrs Pring.

' 'Tis true, indeed. Once she puts reins on a needle, she is
off at a gallop.' He stroked the patch as if it were a piece of
mosaic he was pressing into place. 'Scarce of resources in the
brain-box she may be, but she could mend spiders' webs and
sow a feather back on a bird.'

Mrs Pring, the evening before, had taken a more detached
view of her accomplishments. 'This is the last time, the very
last. I'll not patch his patches no more, not no more.'

I doubted Fr Duddleswell had invited me into his study to
admire Mrs Pring's handiwork, and I was right. 'Father
Neil,' he said, 'there is a shortage of you as there is a glut of
me.' I blinked, then stared. 'You are beginning to look, lad,
as if you were me cheese ration for the week.' I sighed voice-
lessly. It encouraged him to say more emphatically, 'We cannot have you and me doing a Laurel and Hardy on the
parish, you follow? No two ways about it,' he went on in a
biblical vein, 'you must increase and I must decrease. The
lady housekeeper suggests to me that, alas, poor brother, you
need Bovril. In brief, you may be heading for a breakdown.'

So that was what he was wriggling towards. I insisted I had

never felt better in my life.

'Breakdowns in people, as in motor cars, Father Neil, can be very sudden, like. And when an Englishman goes to pieces, 'tis my experience he does so with panache, like a sliced loaf.'

Mrs Pring had reported to him that in a few days' time it was my parents' twenty-fifth wedding anniversary. The day after that was my twenty-fourth birthday. 'I don't know Father Neil, but that you need a holiday. So go home, now, and spend a couple of days in helping your dear ones celebrate.'

Celebrations were not the outstanding feature of our home. We lived happily in Hertfordshire, in the town of Clover Hill, thirty miles north of London. My father was a greengrocer. To the locals, BOYDS was the 'corner shop', which a tall, thin, cloth-capped gentleman, slightly deaf and with a grey brush moustache kept open at all hours.

He had not ever altered in my memory, my father. His habit was to sit sideways at table, invariably with his cap on. He preferred eating with a spoon. He even managed bacon and eggs with a spoon.

He was gruff and of few words. He sometimes shouted at his six children, of whom I was the eldest, but he never laid a finger on us either in anger, or affection. I admired him. More than that, I loved that silent, stubborn man.

Old corduroy trousers under a brown overall. In winter, a sack round his middle and khaki woollen mittens from which protruded raw fingers with nails permanently broken and packed with dirt from shovelling potatoes.

My father never had an assistant in his shop, which was really the converted front room of our house. He couldn't afford an assistant, he said, not with eight mouths to feed. At five o'clock most mornings, rain or shine, he would be off to market or a nearby farm in his old Austin van. Often at night he would be working in the dark 'out the back', shelling peas. He had a talent for buying up sackfuls of peas with sticky pods which no one else wanted, shelling the peas into a bucket and selling them by the pint. The thumb of his right hand, I recall, was nearly always swollen.

We were not exactly the potato-less poor, but economies were his speciality, a kind of art form. He never smoked or drank or drove the van except on business. He never went to the cinema or read a book, and he only turned on the radio for the news, a habit he picked up during the war. Our holidays were walks to a lovely wooded park three miles away on Dad's half-days, where we picnicked when the weather was fine. Our clothes were second hand and hand-ons. It was a case of first up, best dressed. Dad made us use the paper wrapped round oranges for toilet paper.

On Friday nights, Dad took out his orders on a black three-wheeled carrier bike. For an hour or two, one of the children was made to mind the shop and see that no customers duped him into letting them have food on tick when Dad had blacklisted them for not paying their bills.

My father never tried to teach us anything, though he had learned a lot since he finished his schooling at thirteen. If a fuse blew or a tyre punctured or a window was smashed, it was he who mended it – and in secret. He had the unassailable pride of the uneducated man. His children might attend the grammar school and the convent – intellectuals, he called us – but in his house he did all the 'fixing'. He was the boss.

In fact, he was nothing of the sort. It was my mother who made all the major decisions about our schooling and our religion, and about my being sent away to the junior seminary. An inexhaustible fund of affection, she was what our seminary professors called one of the simple faithful. Her faith was as unquestioning as a child's. It was her faith that saw me through the difficult times in the major seminary, especially the first two years. That was when I studied philosophy which was as intelligible to me as Chinese.

My mother was fond of calling to mind her own childhood. Her father was often without work and her mother had to stand at a wash-tub in a laundry from eight in the morning till eight at night for a shilling a day. 'Yet,' my mother said, 'we were happier in those days. Mind you, I wouldn't want them to return.' That was a paradox I could never resolve, for we were happy, too, though we had little enough of the things of the world.

I used to spend my Christmas and summer vacations at home. I was specially close to the youngest of the family, my two sisters, Meg and Jenny. After I was ordained, Mum wanted brother Bob, my junior by two years and a trainee accountant, to give up his attic bedroom to me. She said I needed a quiet room at the top where I could be alone to pray and to say my Office. I preferred to share with Bob, and at nights we talked into the early hours about the past, present and future.

Mum would now ask me to say Grace before and after meals. One look from her made the boss take off his cap, revealing a rare display of white hairs.

The silver wedding anniversary fell on a Sunday. I presided at a solemn sung Mass in the parish church at 11 o'clock. My parents had a special prie-dieu and chair on the sanctuary. Both were in new clothes, bought off the peg. Mother had a trim red hat. Father wore a three-piece suit *and* a new pair of mittens.

When I turned round after the Gospel to read a blessing over them, it was those mittens that made me choke. Not mother's love for us, their joint protection of us, but those mittens and everything they stood for: the lack of opportunity in his life, the long, unbroken, indistinguishable hours, his endurance of ice and cold and grime and dirt without a murmur for us. I blew my nose hard and got a grip on myself. I managed to hold out. Just.

Although I was tired when I returned to St Jude's after our celebration, I was full of joy and gratitude at belonging to such a close knit family.

The parish was in a state of chaos.

'It all began yesterday with the washed Chinese carpet.' Fr Duddleswell pointed grimly to the bare boards in front of the Lady Altar. Lord Mitchin, our richest parishioner, had donated it together with a Persian rug on the sanctuary which had also been stolen. 'Worth £300 the pair, I'd say, Father Neil. I do not know what we are going to do.'

He had called in the police but they were not interested in petty theft. They could not be expected, in any case, to put a round-the-clock watch on every church in the district.

Fr Duddleswell complained that he was not getting the protection he was entitled to as a ratepayer. The first suggestion from the police was that he should lock up the church, outside of services.

'But, Father Neil, we do not want a one-day-a-week church, do we, now? The good people of the parish would not be able to pray in front of the Blessed Sacrament. Think of the Indulgences they would lose.'

The police next proposed that we should take out anything that was movable: carpets, statues, candlesticks, vases, the lot. 'They have no appreciation of the fact that we are *Catholics*, Father Neil. Can our folk be expected to pray without the customary aids to devotion? Indeed they cannot.' He refused to turn his beautiful church into a bare

Protestant meeting hall. 'Who do these bobbies think they are, Father Neil, Henry VIII?'

It appeared the police had no idea who the thief was. It could be a tramp, a gang of kids, a regular criminal. 'In other words, they have about as many clues to our thief's identity,' he said, 'as to that of Jack the Ripper. We can but pray that the thief, whoever he is, turns his attentions elsewhere.'

But the anonymous thief retained his preference for St Jude's. Next day, he struck again. He walked off with a pair of silver candlesticks from the Sacred Heart Altar.

'Where is it going to end?' moaned Fr Duddleswell, when after lunch we witnessed the results of the latest depredations.

He knelt down before the life size statue of the Sacred Heart, saying, 'Let us say a prayer for the criminal, Father Neil.' And he proceeded to gabble, 'Hail Mary, full of grace ... pray for us sinners ... at the hour of our death, Amen.' All this before my knees could touch the floor.

I made a token sign of the cross to show willing. 'What's next, Father?' I asked.

'Doubtless, soon he will be breaking into the boxes.'

This prophecy, too, was fulfilled. That very evening. There were a number of boxes at the back of the church to receive the offerings of the faithful. Boxes for the Poor, the Holy Souls, Catholic Newspapers, Candles, Peter's Pence and Catholic Truth Society pamphlets. The thief showed the catholicity of his tastes. 'He has prized the lid off every one,' roared Fr Duddleswell, boiling with indignation.

I examined the locks and lids and suggested that the thief had used a screw driver.

Fr Duddleswell said, 'We are dealing with a blasphemer, are we not, Father Neil? Not only does he rob the poor and the Holy Father himself, he even breaks open boxes containing money meant for the Holy Souls. And that is a problem on its own.'

I asked him what he meant.

'If the thief stole five shillings from the Holy Souls' Box,' he explained, 'that is the price of a Mass stipend and we ought to say a Mass for the donors' intentions.'

I agreed. It would be terrible if a Holy Soul remained one minute longer in the cleansing fires of purgatory than was strictly necessary because the Mass he was entitled to had not been celebrated. 'I'll offer a Requiem tomorrow, Father.'

'Ah, there, your heart is in the right place, Father Neil. I would offer the same meself but for the fact that I have already promised Janet Murphy to say Mass in the morning for her cat. She is having an operation. A hysterectomy. And she will be lonely, you follow?'

Finding this information highly ambiguous, I said I quite understood he couldn't disappoint Mrs Murphy or her cat.

A locksmith was called in. For £3 he mended the boxes and put a heavy padlock on each. 'That's the best I can do, sirs,' he said, already hinting that his best might not be good enough.

And so it proved. The thief's screw driver managed once more to prize open the boxes without touching the padlocks. This time he had also broken the lock on the baptistery and stolen the casket with the small silver phials of holy oils used for baptisms and anointing the dying.

Fr Duddleswell was crestfallen. It would cost him another £3 to replace the oil stocks and then he'd have to go to the Cathedral to beg for a refill. 'Pray to the Holy Mother,' he counselled me, 'that no one decides to die on us, Father Neil, before a fresh supply of holy oil arrives.'

If that were to happen, I could see myself offering another free Mass for the repose of a brand new Holy Soul.

'God help us, Father Neil, but this thief is a thorn in me eye. He is spoiling me sweet repose and putting the whole of the parish through the mincer.' He decided to draw up a rota of watchers to keep an eye on things, 'as we did during the war, like'.

We were to ask for volunteers on Sunday but in the meantime we would have to take turns ourselves.

'Just you and me?' I asked, wondering whether I could survive vigils of several hours at a stretch. And Sunday was five days away.

'Mrs Pring will be only too glad to help, that's for sure,' he said. 'She has a nose sharper than a briar and more eyes than a fisherman's net. Besides', he added loudly, 'she would far sooner park her bum on a bench than lick this house with a broom.'

Out in the hall, Mrs Pring started up a kind of boating chant. 'Hewing and drawing, cooking and frying, rubbing and scrubbing, washing and drying.'

Fr Duddleswell muttered, 'The voice of the turtle is heard in our land. By the law of averages she was bound sooner or later to blunder into poesie.'

After Mrs Pring had sung her song a few times, she moaned, 'I'm just a beast of burden, I am. A beast of burden.'

'Well, Father Neil,' Fr Duddleswell confided to me, 'she is not Balaam's ass that spoke but once, that's for sure.'

No sooner was Fr Duddleswell's scheme put into operation than I realized its futility. For security reasons, he kept the door leading from the sacristy to the church permanently locked and barred. Whenever a watcher started to open it from the sacristy side, a thief would have half a minute to make his getaway. Another thing, the watcher had to sit or kneel in the benches in front of the boxes so that any prospective thief would see immediately if anyone was on guard.

It was very embarrassing having to turn round whenever a worshipper dropped into church. The faithful resent being spied on by the clergy at their devotions.

Once I tried sitting in the dark of my confessional. Mrs Betty Ryder, President of the Legion of Mary, spied me. She came in and poured out her very fluid soul. After a forty-minute drenching, I chose to sit a couple of rows from the back relying on my ears to warn me if anything out of the ordinary happened.

On Wednesday I ate a big lunch and Fr Duddleswell left me to keep watch while he took his siesta. I must have dozed off because when he came to relieve me at 3.30, red eyed from sleep, not only had the Poor Box been broken into but all the candles had been pinched.

'He must be an indigent eskimo,' observed Fr Duddleswell, when he had made an inventory of our losses, 'but what the mischief came over you, lad?'

I apologized profusely. The thief had been in my grasp and I had let him go.

Fr Duddleswell scratched his forehead and acknowledged the improbability of the thief being so stupid as to return that day. He was wrong. The rest of the boxes were emptied before supper.

'Father Neil, when the bait is worth more than the fish, 'tis time to stop fishing.' After that, he refused to have the boxes mended any more.

I determined to make amends for my unplanned siesta. After supper, I called on Archie Lee, who, as ever, was delighted to see me. From a clothes line by the fireplace hung my pair of pyjamas.

'Sorry Peregrine's out, Father. 'E's gone to Bedford to see 'is old auntie. She's been taken ill.' Anxious not to be caught out in a lie, he told me this was a code for Perry being at the Races. Perry's gambling was the reason he was always skint. He kept back one fiver to wrap round pieces of newspaper and stuffed the lot in his wallet to make himself look plush. 'Sometimes,' complained Archie, 'Perry goes to the gee-gees and leaves me working in a shop all bleedin' day.'

I told Archie I had come to see *him*.

'Another 'orspital job, Father?' said Archie eagerly, rolling up his pyjamas and hiding them under his pillow.

I explained what had been going on in church and said I wanted his help in finding out who the culprit was.

He smiled. 'No trouble there, Father.'

'Not you and Peregrine?' Archie was shocked at the suggestion after he had proved his honesty in so many ways.

'But,' I said after an apology, 'I thought you said you *knew*.'

'Right,' said Archie. 'I'm surprised the fuzz don't. Most like they do but they aint lettin' on.' He explained that every thief is a sort of craftsman with his own little trade marks. 'The marks in this case,' he said, 'is clear as 'is autograph. 'Cept the bloke in question can't write.'

'Will you tell *me* who he is?'

'I might,' said Archie cannily, 'and then I might not.'

'I can't raise much cash this time, Archie. That hospital job cleaned me out.'

'It aint the bread, Father, I just don't wanner grass on one of me old mates. It don't do to shop one of yer own kind.'

I said I fully understood his sense of honour.

'Right, *right*,' reflected Archie, who approved of that way of putting it. 'Also, this bloke is one of us.'

'A con man?'

'You've been and gawn an' done it again,' Archie said reproachfully. 'I mean 'e's an 'oly Roman, like you an' me.'

'That makes it worse.'

'That makes it better—for 'im, I mean,' said Archie. ''E knows 'is way round the church, where all the goodies is, when the boxes is fattest with the lolly an' that type of thin'.'

When I assured him we didn't want to have the thief arrested, Archie relaxed. I knew that when Fr Duddleswell heard the thief was a Catholic, he would want to save him for himself, redeem him, reform him.

''E'll never manage that, Father.'

'Well, at least *stop* him.'

'Even that'll take some doing,' said Archie. 'This gaffer's been pilfering from churches since 'e were six.' It had started when he went to Sunday school. The boxes were crammed after the morning Masses and the habit developed from there. 'Went from strength to strength, see?' I nodded. ''E don't mean no 'arm by it. Knows no different. 'Ow else would 'e eat, tell me that?'

'Either he goes out of business or we do,' I said.

'Bad as that, is it?'

'If I promise we won't "shop" him, Archie, or disclose who put us on to him, will you tell me who he is ... for old time's sake?' I was so excited at the prospect of finding the culprit I was not above a bit of blackmail. Archie hesitated. 'I give you my word that he'll come to no harm, Archie, and we'll do our best to see he gets a chance in life. Like you,' I added.

'Ah,' sighed Archie. 'If only 'e'd go straight like me and Perry, 'E's never 'ad our chance, 'as 'e? And 'e's about as bright in the 'ead as a star by day.'

'This might be his last opportunity, then.'

'It's Bud Norton,' burst out Archie.

'Where does he live?'

''E don't live nowhere. Or, rather, 'e lives everywhere, but not somewhere.'

'No fixed abode.'

'That's what I just said, didn't I? You'd as easy find a wisp of smoke from yesterday's fire.'

I was thinking we would have to catch Bud Norton in the act, after all, when Archie asked if Bud had taken more than money.

'Yes, the silver stocks containing the holy oils.'

'Wicked,' said Archie. 'You'll 'ave to get on 'im before 'e breaks open yer tabernacle. Anythin' else?' I told him the rest. Archie frowned and said, 'Wanner know where to get 'em?'

I could hardly believe my luck. 'You mean you know where Bud Norton keeps his stolen goods?'

' 'E don't keep 'em. 'E passes 'em on to a bloke name of Pedlow in Larkin Street.' Larkin Street was off the King's Road in Chelsea. 'Pedlow buys up everythin' from Bud for a bleedin' song. Real bent, 'e is, and as genuine as a sea breeze off a winkle stall.'

'I'll keep mum, Archie,' I said, touching the side of my nose, 'you can trust Fr Boyd. Oh, yes.'

Next morning after breakfast, while Mrs Pring was keeping watch, I took a bus to the King's Road. Larkin Street had a narrow entrance and was deep in shadow. The only shop in the street was PEDLOW AND SON, FURNITURE DEALERS, EST. 1881.

In the very front row of the window display were our two candlesticks. A notice on them said, PRICELESS SILVERWARE, £35 THE PAIR. I couldn't see the carpets.

Now I'd arrived at the shop, my nerve failed me. There was no sign of an assistant. What if he turned out to be a typical example of the criminal classes and brutally assaulted me?

I plucked up courage, prayed to the Holy Ghost and went in. An old-fashioned bell fixed on top of the door tinkled and I was assailed by the odour of old furniture, mildew and cold stale air.

A white-faced man, about five feet two inches tall, shuffled in from a back room in carpet slippers. He hadn't a hair on his head. A pair of rimless spectacles gave the appearance of a short-sighted egg. He wore, in striking contrast to his face, a black corduroy jacket set off by a drooping black cravat.

Seeing my clerical collar, he broke into a smile. 'James Pedlow, at your service, sir.'

'I've come for the candlesticks in the window.'

'You have admirable taste I *can* see, sir, and an eagle's eye for a bargain, *if* I might say so.' He had a habit of accenting unexpected words. 'Where else *in* London,' he continued, 'could you pick up a pair of antique silver candlesticks *like* that for only £35?'

'I haven't come to buy them, only to claim them,' I said.

'I beg *your* pardon, sir,' said Mr Pedlow, taking one sharp shuffle backwards.

I told him I had come to claim them because they were stolen from our church. His demeanour instantly altered. 'What's your *little* game, then, eh?'

'Game?'

'What are you, a cop?'

'Do I look like one?'

He lifted his spectacles on to his forehead and ran his eye up all six feet and more of me. 'As a *matter* of fact, you do. *Are* you in plain clothes or something?'

Fingering my clerical collar, I replied that I was in my normal uniform.

'You must *be* a con man, then,' he said.

What twisted minds these crooks have, I thought. 'I happen to be a Roman Catholic priest, Mr Pedlow. No,' I added, to forestall a further question, 'this is not a front.'

When he demanded to see identification I realized that I hadn't any except for my name inscribed on my miraculous medal. I didn't think that would do.

'Have you a visiting card?'

'I have only just been appointed to St Jude's and I've not had one printed yet.'

'A driving licence perhaps?'

'I ride a bicycle.'

'A cheque book?'

'I haven't got a bank account.'

This must have been the crushing proof that I was a Catholic priest. He cracked. Like Humpty Dumpty, he was never the same again. 'Well, sir,' he said, bracing himself, 'that's *as* may be. But that gives you no entitlement to claim my candlesticks as your own. I purchased them in good faith *on* the open market.'

I felt my star was in the ascendant. 'You did no such thing,' I affirmed, 'you received them from Bud Norton.'

He cowered in my shadow like a naughty schoolboy. 'That's the first time in twenty years Bud's grassed on me.'

'He didn't,' I said. 'I got a tip-off.' Those Hollywood gangster movies were proving useful.

'An enemy has done this,' he said, sounding quite biblical to my ears.

'It doesn't matter who did it, it's done,' I cried, 'and I demand my candlesticks back, otherwise I'll prosecute you for theft.'

'Theft!' exclaimed Mr Pedlow, riled by the word. 'Theft! I have never stolen anything *in* my life.'

'To receive or retain what you know belongs to another is as much theft as if you had taken it yourself. Whoever steals through another is himself a thief.' Moral theology had its uses, too.

Mr Pedlow appeared to think I was quoting from a law book. 'How *can* you prove they belong to you?' he asked more respectfully.

Time for my trump card. 'Here,' I said, pulling out a picture from my inside pocket, 'is a photo of those candlesticks in the place Bud Norton stole them from: the Sacred Heart Altar.'

He didn't even bother to look. 'They're yours,' he said miserably.

My triumph could not have been more complete if I had pulled a gun on him. 'Do you want me to call the cops?' I thundered, revelling in my role of bully-boy.

'What's up?' he said timorously. 'Didn't you hear *me* say they're yours?'

'The carpets. I want them back, too.'

'Which ones, sir?'

'Chinese and Persian.'

'Come with me, sir,' he said with a gesture of defeat.

I followed him into the back room and searched a tall pile of carpets till I found the two belonging to St Jude's. 'Finally,' I said greedily, 'where are the candles?'

'I don't stock candles.'

That jogged my memory. 'Forget the candles.' I could afford to be generous. 'Where are the stocks with the holy oils?'

He knew exactly what I meant. He crossed to a cupboard and drew out the casket with the three silver phials. As if despairing of mankind, I asked, 'What possible use could anyone have found for these?'

'They would *have* made such nice snuff boxes,' he whimpered.

I struggled with the stolen goods up to the King's Road where I stopped a taxi. As luck would have it, out of the hundreds of cabbies in London, it had to be the one who had taken me and my bike home in less happy circumstances. He took one look at my haul of furniture and said, 'Don't tell me. St Jude's.'

When Fr Duddleswell saw his precious possessions, he raised his eyes to heaven, saying, '*Magnificat anima mea Dominum.*' Then in a more earthly tone: 'So you tracked him down, Father Neil?'

'It's useful having one or two contacts in the underworld, Father.' I proceeded to tell him the whole story, adding a spice of drama here and there, but leaving out the thief's name. 'That,' I said, 'is a professional secret.'

'You cannot even tell me his initials?' I shook my head.

He didn't press the point. Once he knew the thief was an R.C. he felt a special responsibility towards him. Besides, to take him to court would only bring Holy Mother Church into disrepute.

'Shall I take the carpets and candlesticks into the church, Father?' I asked. It seemed clear to me that if the thief were to see them there, he would know we were on to him and leave us in peace.

Fr Duddleswell didn't agree. On past evidence, the thief was quite capable of stealing them and offering them again to the Chelsea fence. He had devised his own method of stopping the thief's tricks. 'Come with me, Father Neil, and I will show you something that escaped me notice before.'

In the church, Mrs Pring was keeping solitary vigil. He put her on guard outside so that the burglar would not be tempted to enter and went up ahead of me into the organ loft.

'Well, Father Neil, we never thought to keep a look-out up here, did we?'

The loft overhangs the back of the church. 'But this is no use,' I said, peering over the wooden balustrade. 'We've no view of the boxes from here.' This was why we had discounted the place as a watchtower in the first place.

Fr Duddleswell drew my attention to the back of the loft. 'Look down there.' In the floorboards was a crack half an inch thick. 'Here,' he said, 'we can see without being seen.'

I made the point that by the time we clattered down the spiral stairs the thief would be further away than the Houses of Parliament.

'Ah, to be sure. But since he is a Catholic, Father Neil, we are not aiming to nab him. Only reform him. And,' he said mysteriously, 'we will accomplish that without laying a finger on his person, without so much as letting him set eyes on us.'

He outlined his plan. In our parish lived Paul J. Bentley, a radio actor in the B.B.C.'s drama company. The idea was to get him to put a message on tape. When the thief appeared, we would play this message very loudly from our hiding place in the loft.

Within twenty-four hours, the recording was in our hands. In Fr Duddleswell's study it sounded stupendous. A B.B.C. engineer had added a sinister echo effect.

Fr Duddleswell was to have the tape recorder all warmed up, and when Bud Norton came in, I was to give a signal. He only needed to release the pause button and Bud would get the message.

Next morning at eleven, after we had been watching for an hour, an elderly, balding gentleman in a black overcoat appeared. He sank to his knees in silent prayer for fully five minutes. I had seen enough of life lately not to be taken in by pious attitudes. When he rose, looked around him furtively to see no one was looking and crossed to the Poor Box, I gave Fr Duddleswell the agreed signal. The recorder gave out a full blast:

'THIEVES WHO ARE UNREPENTANT WILL PERISH ... PERISH ... PERISH ...'

The natural echo of the building intensified the ghostly echo on the tape. It chilled me to the marrow. Fr Duddleswell pressed the pause button down and we kept quite still, scarcely daring to breathe.

Below there was no sound. Puzzled by the silence, I peeped through the crack in the floorboards to find that the thief had returned to his place and was once more lost in contemplation. His conversion must have been as sudden as St Paul's. I beckoned Fr Duddleswell to me. He tiptoed across and put his eye to the crack.

'Holy Jesus,' he whispered, putting a shaky finger to his lips. ' 'Tis Lord Mitchin himself. Deaf as a trumpet. He cannot be wearing his hearing-aid today.'

'Lucky for us,' I whispered back.

'*Deo* bloody *gratias*,' he said, signing himself.

When after a quarter of an hour, Lord Mitchin left, Fr Duddleswell wound the tape back. I asked him if we should go on with it.

'How else, Father Neil, are we to recover one of Christ's lost sheep, tell me that, now?'

I went back to my post and Fr Duddleswell bent down, his finger poised to release the button. There was a clatter of feet. This time, when I looked through the chink in the floor, there was this shabby, shifty looking character. Bud Norton for sure. An army greatcoat reached to his ankles. Beneath it was a pair of shoes without toecaps and with string for laces. On his hands he wore a pair of khaki mittens.

Bud made no pretence of praying. He simply stood there, his face raised and his body arched like a squirrel's, listening. I saw his grimy bald head, his grizzled face, his red-rimmed watery eyes. My heart, in a mad gallop, went out to him. It was the mittens that did it.

Until this moment, Bud Norton had been a shadow among shadows, a thief, a nuisance, a name stirred half jokingly into conversations. Now here he was, a common, shameless, pitiable vagrant who walked the streets in toeless shoes by day and slept where he could at nights. 'As bright in the 'ead as a star by day,' as Archie in his mercy put it, and as much soft flesh and warm blood as Fr Duddleswell or I.

Bud went over to the Poor Box. A rusty screwdriver was in his hand. Out of the corner of my eye, I saw Fr Duddleswell getting tense as he waited for my signal. It was cowardly of me but I gave it.

The ugly sound from the tape-recorder reverberated round the church. Bud stood there paralysed.

'Once more?' Fr Duddleswell mouthed in my direction.

I nodded and the next message must have gone right to the heart of poor, old Bud Norton.

'THOU SHALT NOT STEAL ... STEAL ... STEAL ...'

I saw Bud start and shiver, and I heard him say in a hoarse whisper, 'Godalmighty!' Then something which, together with his mittens, broke me up. He genuflected. The next moment, he was gone.

In the organ loft, we both stayed motionless for a while. I closed my eyes, only opening them when I felt Fr Duddleswell's hand on my shoulder.

'Get up, lad,' he said gently. 'I feel the same as you. 'Tis a dangerous game, playing God, to be sure, even to put a stop to a man's thieving.' He stood up. 'I only barked so I would not have to bite. But I should have devised another scheme.'

Fr Duddleswell was at last able to have the locks on the boxes fixed permanently. Together we combed the district looking for Bud for three days till late in the evening. We called in at the local Doss House and the Salvation Army Hostel. One old dosser, reeking of methylated spirits, claimed to have seen Bud three days before but not since. 'Imagine,' said Fr Duddleswell, 'no one has so much as heard a taste of him.'

It was cold and wintering early. The Lord had started to shake his salt-cellar over the nights and mornings. I was wobbly on my feet as if I was heading for a bout of 'flu and Fr Duddleswell confessed to feeling as wretched as a Christmas without snow.

We were forced to conclude that Bud had moved away. In a last desperate effort at atonement I persuaded Fr Duddleswell to come with me to Archie Lee's. Archie was on his own, eating lunch. He pointed to his poached eggs on toast. 'Adam and Eve on a raft,' he said, laughing.

When I put Archie in the picture, he asked what day it was. I said it was Saturday. No, he wanted to know the day of the month. November 30th.

'And what's the hour?' asked Archie.

In exasperation, I said, '12.45.'

'Then,' said Archie glumly, 'I can't 'elp yer, 'cept to tell you 'e could be an 'undred miles away by now.' The only predictable thing about Bud Norton was that he only stayed one month in any district. On the last day of the month, before midday, he was off. 'By tonight,' said Archie, ' 'e could be in Land's End or John o' Groats.'

That was that. Fr Duddleswell shook Archie's hand papering the palm with a pound note and we walked slowly home to St Jude's.

Before we went into the presbytery, Fr Duddleswell suggested we pray for Bud in front of the Blessed Sacrament. Neither of us could have guessed when the whole miserable business began how overjoyed we would be to find that for the last time the boxes had been rifled.

Nine

SEX BOWS ITS LOVELY HEAD

During the night I could hear awful howls and screams. In a daze, I kept asking myself if it was the wind, or had a huge dog been let loose in the alley? It occurred to me that I might be responsible for the noise but that was impossible, I was in no pain.

I was a tall tree which a lumberjack felled with a single stroke of the axe and lifted up in one hand and felled again. Each time I hit the ground my body shook and threatened to disintegrate.

I was dreaming and in my dream I was by the sea and the racket I had heard was the wind and waves pounding the shore and there was salt spray on my face and lips and I slipped on the rocks and fell into black waters and was drowning.

The room was an orange split down the middle. Red, molten light was shaken on to my eyeballs. Fr Duddleswell, a total stranger in his dressing gown. Mrs Pring in spectral curlers and hairnet. The pugnacious smell of whisky, and Dr Daley with a halo like a blister round his entire head was wheezing something about pneumonia and hospital.

I desperately wanted to help whoever was ill but I could not shake myself awake. I was still drowning, slowly but surely. The river-bed of my throat was as narrow and clogged as a capillary tube.

Now I was on my back in a hammock. There were fireflies

in the night sky and a long white liquid road stretched up to the moon.

'A hundred and two, Father.'

Was I as old as that? Nurse Owen had not aged and here was I all of a sudden one hundred and two.

'It's going down, Father,' Nurse Owen said. And so was I, coughing my dry cough, and going down, down, down, into the waters.

Dr Daley, half drunk, was still a good diagnostician. I had pneumonia. I came round in the amenity room where I had cured but failed to convert Mr Bwani.

For a few days I had terrible pains in the chest and a fever. Nurse Owen sweetened every aspect of my discomfort. Ever by my side, she soothed my brow, took my temperature and held my wrist to try to catch up with my racing pulse. I fervently wished Archie had not walked off with my best pair of pyjamas.

When I could breathe more deeply again, there followed days of bewildering happiness. Nurse Owen was giving me more of her time, I was convinced, than I was entitled to as a mere patient. The amenity room made it possible for us to talk in a quiet, natural way. About our work, mainly.

On her day off, when I did not see her, the hours limped along like wounded grasshoppers. Feeling sorry for myself, I reflected that I had passed my life in entirely male dominated surroundings since I was fourteen. That was when I entered the junior seminary. My mother and sisters apart, women had only walked on the horizon of my world. I had never taken a girl to the cinema, or been to a dance. I went to my last party at the age of twelve.

I had no female friends of any sort. Yes, I was chaplain to the Legion of Mary. Most members were pop-eyed, middle-aged ladies who talked world without end about 'true Marian devotion'.

I was welcomed as a polite, anonymous stranger at many a hearth. But to no one could I allow myself the luxury of saying who I was. To them I was Melchizedek: no father or mother or brothers or sisters or antecedents. Worse, no present feelings and no future hopes.

'Give me, good Lord,' I prayed each night with Lacordaire, 'a heart of flesh for charity and a heart of steel for chastity.' Outside the amenity room, I felt my life was becoming steelier and lonelier every day.

When Fr Duddleswell and Mrs Pring visited me, bearing gifts like the Magi, I kept saying I was very keen to return to work. Mrs Pring arranged the chrysanthemums while Fr Duddleswell opened up the Get Well cards in between swallowing my grapes. 'By the time you leave here, Father Neil,' he said, his mouth full of purple mush, 'provided they do not starve your plate, like, your shadow should be considerably fatter.'

How could I tell this quaint, benign couple that in the centre of my being I never wanted to quit the Kenworthy General?

Fr Duddleswell suggested I be transferred to the private hospital run by nuns where the sick clergy of the diocese were usually treated. I would not hear of him being put to any inconvenience. Nor did I want to convalesce in a rest home by the sea, also run by the good sisters.

After that, no further attempts were made to evict me from Paradise.

Once or twice I asked myself if that strange flutter in the region of my stomach when Nurse Owen held my hand was the stirrings of love. I put it out of my mind. Fr Duddleswell was bringing me Holy Communion every morning at first light and I was keen to be worthy of the Lord's coming.

Such bliss could not last. The dark day came when the doctor signed my discharge. I was free to go home. It was more like a sentence of perpetual banishment.

Half an hour before Fr Duddleswell came to collect me, Nurse Owen appeared and shyly thanked me for being a model patient.

'I'm very grateful, Nurse,' I said 'for *everything*.' She shrugged and smiled as if to say it was all in the course of duty. 'Anyway, Nurse, I'll see you around the ward before long.' However long would be too long.

She left to attend to a fat Greek boy nomel Nicos who had developed a fever after having his appendix out. Happy. happy Nicos.

For a few days, Fr Duddleswell 'adamantinely' refused to let me loose on the parish. During my enforced confinement I tried to sort out my ambiguous relationship with Nurse Owen. Was her shyness really coyness, or was it respect for the priesthood? What did I feel for her? Did she feel anything for me? With such questioning, the mornings no longer came before my head hit the pillow at night. Hours pretended they were months. I was afraid to go into the kitchen at night for tea in case the police should invade the place.

Nothing had been resolved by the time I resumed my chaplaincy work. All I knew was I wanted to talk to Nurse Owen privately from time to time. I would ask her if she was of the same mind.

I walked up the staircase to Prince Albert Ward with a thumping head. Fortunately, she was alone in Sister's office writing up her reports.

'Hello, Nurse.' I smiled nervously.

She beamed back at me. 'Fr Boyd, how nice to see you up and about.'

I judged her welcome to be more than friendly. She was aglow. If I did not say quickly what I had prepared I would never say it.

'Nurse Owen.'

'Yes, Father?'

'Nurse, I feel really indebted to you for all you have done for me.' She cast her lovely brown eyes downwards, without a word. 'I was wondering, Nurse, if I might ask you a personal question.'

The Holy Ghost must have been on my side at that moment. I saw she was wearing a diamond ring. I pointed to it stricken, but smiling bravely.

'Yes, Jeremy ... that is, Dr Spinks, has asked me to marry him. We became engaged last Saturday.' She began twirling the thing round her finger in front of me. 'I shouldn't be wearing it really while I'm on duty, Father, but it is still such a novelty.'

'Congratulations,' I said, commiserating with myself. With all the lucidity of mind keen pain can bring I added, 'As I was saying, Nurse, I want to give you a box of chocolates and I'd like to know the sort you like best.'

'Oh, Black Magic are my favourites.'

'You are sure you didn't mind me asking?' I added confusedly.

'Not in the least.'

'Fine, well, Nurse, if you'll allow me, I'll bring you ... and Dr Spinks ... a pound box of Black Magic next time I pass this way.'

I left Kenworthy General without attending to a single patient.

*　　　*　　　*

175

I was hurt. I was humiliated. I was angry. At first I wondered why she had gone out of her way to be so nice to me. What made *her* think she could be nice to me? Soon I realized I was being stupid. Why should Nurse Owen single me out for an uncharacteristic attack of nastiness?

Guilt waxed in me as anger waned. I started to blame myself. I knew that if I wasn't careful I'd blame myself too much and accuse myself of impure thoughts and desires. If that happened, I would find myself in the altogether murkier realm of mortal sin which, as I had told Mrs Rollings, required confession – number and species. It was wiser to forget the whole affair.

But my conscience gave me no peace. What if I was no longer in a state of grace and making things worse by celebrating Mass and administering the sacraments when I needed absolution myself?

I had to get it off my chest. I did not want to trouble my normal confessor at the Cathedral who knew me for my laziness, exaggerations and impatience. I chose to pop along instead to a nearby Jesuit House of Studies and confess to a priest who did not know me from Adam.

One morning at ten o'clock, I plucked up courage and rang the bell. A Brother with a club foot opened the door. 'Come for confession, Father?' Was guilt written so large on my face that a total stranger could read it at once? 'No one here at the moment, save Fr Strood. An American, Father. But I dare say if you're in a hurry.' I said I was. 'Second Floor, Room 12, then. There's no phone in his room so you'll just have to go on up.'

I knocked on Room 12 and was greeted by a loud, drawling, 'Come in, please.' The voice was Jimmy Cagney in a friendly mood.

I opened the door only to recoil in horror. There in the

176

middle of the room was a crew-cut, middle-aged gentleman clad only in the briefest of blue underpants. He was holding a towel but not for protection.

'I'm sorry to disturb you,' I said.

'What makes you think you're disturbing *me*? I was about to freshen up, that's all.' Sensing my embarrassment, he added, 'I *am* wearing my fig leaf.'

'I was looking for a priest,' I stammered, 'for confession.'

'That's okay, Father, you've found one. Only too glad to oblige.' He promptly collapsed on to a chair, put the towel round his neck like a stole and motioned to me to kneel beside him. 'Ready?' he said. 'Shoot.'

I told him it was four days since my last confession. 'Great, Father,' he smiled, 'glad to know you frequent the sacrament. Now, what's on your mind?'

I explained as best I could my feelings towards the Nurse who had looked after me, first of tenderness and lately of bitterness.

'Gee,' he said, tugging on the ends of his towel and then scratching his hairy chest. 'I've been hospitalized three times in seven years and I've fallen in love with my nurse *every* time, can you imagine? *Different* ones at that. I guess I'm just *promiscuous*.' He paused as if contemplating the pretty faces of all the nurses whose hands he had been through. 'Plan to see her again, Father?'

I answered that I was bound to see her on my rounds but she had become engaged to a doctor. 'That's probably what made me so sore,' I admitted.

'I *read* you, Father. Anything else?' I hadn't prepared anything else. 'Okay, Father, tell the good Lord you're sorry for all the sins of your past life. For your penance, I want you to pray that your nurse friend will be very happy.' Through two or three camel-like yawns, he gave me absolution.

As I stood up, he grabbed me by the hand and squeezed it till it hurt. 'Frank Strood from Jersey City,' he said, grinning from ear to ear. 'And you, do you have a name, too?' I wasn't used to shaking hands with underpanted Jesuits but I told him who I was. 'Great to meet you, Neil. See you again, I hope.'

'Thank you, Father,' I said, retreating to the door. I was afraid that if I didn't get out in a hurry he might want to confess his promiscuities to me. 'You've been extremely helpful, Father.'

He waved the towel after me like a handkerchief. 'Think nothing of it. Bye, now, Neil. Bye.'

'Here are the chocolates, Nurse. Sorry I didn't remember them before.' Lies. I had thought of nothing but her and her chocolates for days.

She thanked me, adding out of politeness, 'I'd forgotten all about them, Father.'

With a bitterness that surprised me, I thought, 'I bet you did.'

To prove to her and myself that I had no designs on her I had bought her a half pound box of Cadbury's Milk Tray. She seemed pleased all the same as she clutched them to her breast.

'Father,' she said, 'I was wondering if you could possibly help me' – oh, yes – 'help *us*' – oh, no. 'Jeremy and I are planning to marry next spring.' Remembering the confessor's admonition I wished her every happiness.

She had been told that Jeremy had to have three or four instructions before marriage.

'He's not a Catholic, then, I take it, Nurse?'

'Jeremy's not anything.' It staggered me that a beautiful, devout, apparently intelligent Catholic should contemplate giving herself away to a self-confessed pagan. 'It helps, doesn't it, Father,' she asked eagerly, 'him not believing in anything?'

'I suppose so,' I replied. 'It means he won't object to the children being Catholics.'

Her rose-like face rushed into full bloom at the mention of children. I explained that non-Catholics had to sign in advance a promise that all children born of the union will be baptized and brought up in the Catholic faith. This seemed to upset her.

'Look, Nurse, he's not likely to raise any objections, is he? You made the point yourself he hasn't any faith.'

'No, Father, but he does have very strong convictions.'

Blind prejudice, I thought, and nothing more. I said, 'Presumably, he'll want you to follow your conscience?'

'What about *his* conscience? What if he wants ... any children born of the union ... to decide for themselves when they're old enough?'

'Awkward,' I said unsympathetically.

Nurse Owen looked irresistible as she clutched her small box of chocolates to her heaving bosom. 'That's why I was looking to you for help, Father. Could you have a meal with us?'

This was rubbing salt in the wound. 'When's best for you, Nurse?' She mentioned Friday evening at 8. My diary was blank on that day but a streak of perversity made me say, 'Sorry I can't make that evening. The Friday after is all right.'

She was so grateful and so quintessentially nice that if I'd had the talent I would have kicked my own backside. By eating at her place I would at least be spared having to share the bill. I was beginning to think that curates don't get paid nearly enough for all they have to suffer.

'Flat 6A, Flood Court,' she said. 'I share with a secretary. She goes out Friday evenings, so we can have a quiet meal, just the three of us.'

The prospect of instructing Dr Spinks on the rights and duties of marriage made me nervous. He had seen sex in the raw, I had only met it in Brown's four volumes of *Moral Theology*. There all the spicy bits had been put into Latin, presumably so that inquisitive lay folk could not read it. Unfortunately, I was never very good at Latin.

Apart from Brown, there were only two ways we seminarists had been formally instructed on sex.

One was when Canon Flynn, our Professor, called us up two by two to his dais in the lecture room. This was in our fifth year. Spread out on his desk was a battered old tome with two sectional drawings, suitably distanced, of the '*Respective Anatomies*'. The text was in French, the parts were listed in Latin. To cap it all, sectional drawings, even of cars and aeroplanes, never meant anything to me.

The Canon darted here and there with his long pencil, taking care not to touch the page. He hurriedly gave the names and functions of various arcane organs which Brown had referred to in a lump as *membra minus honesta*.

'Any questions?'

There were never any questions. The chief point of seminary training was that you should know all the answers and none of the questions. It was all over in forty-five seconds.

In our sixth and final year, any gaps in our knowledge of sex and procreation were to be filled by Father Head, a Scottish priest who had been a surgeon before his ordination.

He turned out to be the leanest, most highly strung individual I have ever seen. He stood at the blackboard, from which were hung enormous charts, red-faced and quivering, and proceeded to describe the act of intercourse as if it were a torrid, North African tank battle between Rommel and Montgomery.

I remember Jimmy Farrelly, the wag of the year, declaring afterwards, 'Jesus! I still can't figure out who won.'

I was in dire need of help when I went to Fr Duddleswell's study. He was engrossed in a tabloid newspaper which he bought regularly for Mrs Pring. He looked up at me and tutted: 'Father Neil, newspapers these days. 'Tis all bosoms and etceteras. Cast your eye over this.'

The picture in the centre spread was of a pretty girl in a nothing dress. The caption was *Thigh Priestess*. He was at a loss to know why the media chose to advertise those parts of the human person so devoid of interest that previous generations had refrained from showing them at all.

'Seen one, seen 'em all,' he said. 'Like elbows. D'you not think, Father Neil, that sex is a bit like the aroma of coffee. It promises far more than it can possibly deliver.'

I decided to take his word for it and nodded agreement.

He asked, 'Be honest, now, can you imagine any sane individual getting titillation from the likes of *this*?'

'No, Father,' I gulped, amazed at what age does to a man. I told him I had a mixed marriage arranged for the new year and wanted to know how to go about it.

He went across to his filing cabinet for the forms. The most important was the dispensation form for disparity of cult. The non-Catholic had to sign promising never to interfere with the faith of the Catholic partner and to allow the children to be brought up in the true faith.

I told him the bride was a nurse and the groom a non-Catholic doctor from the K.G. 'Well, Father Neil,' he said, 'be sure to put him right about birth-control, divorce, abor-

tion and things of that sort.' I was particularly to stress the
Church's teaching on contraception. Sex is not a child's play-
thing. It is a most marvellous mechanism for the manufac-
ture of children. In this, he continued to inform me, men as
far apart as Gandhi and Bernard Shaw were in agreement
with the Church. Birth-control usually meant no birth and
no control.

I asked whether the dispensation was granted easily. 'No
trouble these days,' he replied, 'provided there is a reason for
the marriage. Is the girl pregnant, for instance?'

'I shouldn't think so,' I said, biting my lip to hide my
indignation.

'Better check, Father Neil. Pregnancy is by far the most
acceptable of the canonical reasons. Then there is *firmum
propositum nubendi*, a firm determination to marry.'

I acknowledged grudgingly that she had that. 'What I
mean is,' he explained, 'would she marry in the Register
Office if the Church refused her a dispensation?' I said I
guessed not because she's a pious Catholic. 'If we are not
careful,' he winked mischievously, 'she will prove to be too
pious and we will find *no* canonical pretext for marrying her
off. Is she *super-adulta*, now?'

'What is over-age, Father?'

'Twenty-four. Any girl above that is reckoned to have distinctly reduced chances of marrying. That is why the Church
allows a dispensation, especially if she has a face like an old
boot into the bargain.'

Seeing I was stunned at what constituted advanced years
in a woman, he explained that the law was made with Latin
ladies, fed on a diet of spaghetti Bolognese, in mind. 'They
are mostly blown like autumn roses before our own women
are in bud, you follow? But if canon law works to our advantage in this instance, why complain?'

I said that the girl in question couldn't be more than twenty-two and was not really ugly, so I supposed, almost joyfully, that was the end of it.

'Nothing of the sort, Father Neil,' he came back, dashing my last hope. 'The matter is exceedingly simple. Do not forward the application for a dispensation till the last minute and plead *omnia parata*. You tell the Chancellor of the diocese that everything is ready for the wedding and it would cause a ripe shemozzle if at this late hour 'twere to be called off.'

I put it to him that canon lawyers would find a loophole to let Satan have a holiday from Hell.

'Father Neil, the Church has all the loving deviousness of a mother, if you are still with me.' I had to make sure the forms were filled in but not dated. If I reminded him to countersign them four days before the wedding, he would pass them on to the Chancellor himself. 'And warn that young medic, mind, I want no hanky-panky over birth-control.'

With polished shoes and brushed suit I rat-tatted on the door of Flat 6A. Nurse Owen, her long red hair cascading on to her shoulders, answered my knock clad in a long cherry-coloured dress. I admired the propriety of its high neckline.

Spinks was a mess in sandals, jeans and open-necked shirt. The only bosom on show was his.

'Jerry it is,' he said in a friendly tone. Since he already knew my name I shook his hand in silence. 'Glad Sarah could persuade you to come.'

Sarah. Sarah Owen. What a lovely name.

'Our paths have hardly crossed,' Dr Spinks went on, 'since you cured that chap from the Gold Coast.'

He actually had a small bald patch on top, the size of a

florin. What was Sarah up to, hitching herself to a prematurely balding pagan? The Church really shouldn't be so liberal with her dispensations.

'Talk to Father, Jeremy,' urged Sarah, 'while I put the finishing touches to the meal.'

When she went to the kitchen, Dr Spinks said, 'Beer?'

'No thanks.'

'Sherry?' I shook my head. 'You *will* have a glass of wine with your meal?'

'Please.'

He looked relieved that I had some weaknesses. 'Tricky business, Fr Boyd, putting down the anchor.'

It was in his favour that he had addressed me correctly. 'I'm sure,' I said.

A black hole yawned in the conversation. Then he asked me if I would like a disc put on. I tried to shake myself out of my boorish mood and failed. 'Not particularly.'

Sarah must have had her ear pinned to the door. She returned and thrust a plate in front of me. 'Have a crisp, Father. And here's the cheese dip.' One glance at Dr Spinks told him, no discs tonight.

'Marriage is a sacrament, isn't it, Father?' she said. 'Jeremy is ever so keen to know what that means, aren't you Jeremy?'

I was happy to be on home ground. I replied that it is a sacrament provided both partners are baptized.

'You *have* been baptized, haven't you, Jeremy?'

Dr Spinks said 'yes, love' but he had repudiated all that when he was twelve. I insisted that if he had been baptized, he was in some marginal sense a Christian, and if he married another Christian it would be a sacrament.

'Whether I like it or not?'

'Yes,' I said aloud, and inwardly, whether you damn well like it or not. He asked what follows from that. 'To begin with,' I answered, 'when the marriage has been consummated, there's no possibility of a divorce.'

'Consummated?' He spoke it plainly as a four syllable word. 'Just once?' I nodded. 'Bloody hell,' he laughed, winking at Sarah, 'only once *after* we're married and it's till death us do part.'

Sarah turned the colour of her dress and retreated into the kitchen. Was he such a swine as to cast aspersions on his fiancée's honour?

Through avocado pear, plaice and chips, and apple pie it was sex and marriage. Dr Spinks was against everything the Church stood for on moral issues. He argued the reasonableness of abortion if the prognosis is that the baby's likely to be born deformed or the mother's life is in danger. Likewise in cases of rape.

I did not care to pursue this topic over fish and chips but I made my position clear. God infuses the soul at conception and so the child in the womb has all the rights of a human being.

For him, talk about murdering embryos was mere rhetoric. The Church's teaching on birth-control was plain daft. 'I've been researching into women's periods,' he announced to Sarah's discomfort. 'I've had the nurses at the K.G. and half the girls from the Teachers' Training College keeping charts and thermometer checks.'

Sarah stood up to remove the dirty dishes. 'Cheese and biscuits to follow.'

'I even asked Norah if she'd care to take part,' Dr Spinks went on. 'Just to flatter her, of course.'

The conclusion of his survey was that women are about as reliable as the English weather. My experience of Sarah had taught me that already.

'Did you know, Father,' he confided in a boozy stage

whisper, 'Sarah is one of my menstrual girls?' He roared with laughter and overturned his glass of Beaujolais. 'Her cycles are so irregular, I call her Penny-Farthing. One is thirty-three days, the next is eighteen.' My right hand was volunteering to punch his nose.

He started dabbing up the wine with his table napkin. 'Just my luck to be marrying the most inconsistent girl in the whole bloody troupe. Her only safe period will be from fifty-five to ninety.' He chuckled at his own joke. 'I tell you this in strictest confidence. If, as your Church seems to want, I'm limited to every inconceivable opportunity, I might as well become one of the *castrati* in the heavenly choir.' He dug me in the ribs. 'Like you, old pal.'

I should not have come. There was always the risk of this detestable chumminess.

'Safe period,' Dr Spinks mocked. 'I heard your Church was against sex before marriage but denying it to a randy fellow *after* marriage is bloody ridiculous. Encourages infidelity.' Then without respite, 'And why should a celibate presume to instruct me on sex? It's as lunatic as allowing only orphans to be Marriage Counsellors.'

I was about to push his face in when the key turned in the lock. Sarah rushed in from the kitchen crying, 'Oh, no!'

A young woman was at the head of eight of nine dishevelled youngsters. All were loaded down with tins, bottles and French loaves.

'Debbie,' said Sarah, wringing her hands, 'you told me you were at Jane's for the evening.'

'We were, Sarah darling, but her parents returned unexpectedly from Sunderland. Puritans the pair of them. They even lock up the beds while they're away.'

Sarah introduced me to her flatmate. 'Debbie Shackles, Fr Boyd.'

186

'He's cute,' said Debbie, pursing her lips in a lewd fashion. 'Shake.'

A tousle-haired lad, looking like a pearly king in a black leather jacket sewn with silver buttons, caught sight of me. 'Sarah,' he rejoiced, 'you didn't tell us you were having a fancy-dress.'

Someone put on a jazz record and several started to bob and weave. Johnny, the lad who imagined I was all dressed up, pointed to where a girl had parked herself on the floor and was gazing blankly like a guru into space. 'Rebecca Sacks, Reverend. She's high.'

'I'm Roman Catholic,' I said.

'Care for a puff?' Johnny asked, after exhaling meticulously.

'No thanks, I don't smoke.'

'Sticking to cigarettes, eh?'

I went across to Rebecca and tried to shake her hand. It felt broken. 'Fr Boyd,' I said.

'Tweet-tweet.' She flapped her arms pathetically.

'My!' yelled Johnny from across the room. 'You've really made a hit with Becky, man. Stay with it and she's a regular communicant.'

Sarah took my arm and steered me towards the door. 'Father,' she said, 'I'm terribly sorry about this.'

'Don't apologize,' I shouted above the din.

As she let me out, Sarah was saying, 'You will come again, won't you, Father? If you talk to Jeremy long enough, he's bound to come round to our way of thinking.'

I was still licking my wounds next morning when the phone rang. A raucous voice: 'Jack Hately, here. My wife needs to be anointed. Come quick, Father.'

The phone went dead before I could ask the caller for his

address. I rushed down to Fr Duddleswell's study. He wasn't there. I raced to the kitchen to ask Mrs Pring if she could identify the caller.

Calmly, without raising her eyes from her ironing, she said, 'The Hatelys? Yes. They're on Fr D's side of the parish.' Mrs Hately had been seriously ill for years and Fr Duddleswell anointed her every month to be on the safe side.

'I'd better go along all the same, Mrs P.'

'Wouldn't if I were you. Fr D'll be back within the hour and he'll go himself.'

'You're *not* me,' I retorted, 'and I'm going.'

'Suit yourself,' said Mrs Pring with a toss of her head. '3 Springfield Road.'

I cycled there at speed. Effects of bombing were still to be seen in the battered buildings and vacant housing lots.

Number 3 was now the end house. Hardly a house. It was a basement, its outer wall buttressed by wooden beams sunk in the ground.

I knocked three or four times, louder and louder, until a woman's voice cried out, 'Jack, a visitor, a *visitor*!' and an old chap beyond the biblical span hobbled to the door. He had a loud, hollow voice. 'Is Fr Duddles away? You'll have to do, then.'

Behind him, propped up on a large, brass bed was his wife, her yellow-white hair splayed across a discoloured pillow. Desolation. Water dripping into a pitted zinc basin, shelves in disarray, greasy gas cooker, an ancient iron bath-tub, the pervasive smell of an old person's untended sick room.

'You the new curate?' Mrs Hately enquired hoarsely. 'I can see all the girls falling for you.' She was a flirt. 'You're easy on the eye. Much nicer'n my Jack.' I looked at Jack and marvelled at the minuteness of the compliment. 'I keep telling Jack, I do so admire men with thick wavy hair.'

Her bald-headed Jack nodded and smiled inanely. Only a deaf man could have absorbed so many insults without protest.

I asked Mrs Hately about her health. 'Haven't been well for centuries,' she replied.

'There, there,' boomed Jack in what was meant to be a soothing tone.

'First my arthritis, Father, and now'—indicating the faulty organ—'my heart.'

'There, there, me darlin'.'

I took out the holy oils. 'Fr Duddles,' she said, 'anointed me last week.'

'There, there,' sounded the drum.

'Oh, shut up, Jack, won't you?' she yelled at him. He smiled until he saw her grimacing. 'The anointing don't help me none,' she croaked. 'I'm a condemned building. Jack's done it. He'll be the death of me.' Jack smiled slyly and toothlessly from the far side of the room. 'The Church is taking my Jack away from me.'

What did she mean? What possible use would the Church find for dear old Jack?

'He's just longing for me to drain away and die, Father. So's he can return to the bosom of Holy Mother Church.'

Jack or Mrs Hately or both must have been married before. That made their present marriage invalid in the Church's eyes. If Mrs Hately died, Jack would be free to return to the sacraments.

I jumped to Jack's defence but she was not listening. 'Been together more'n forty years,' she moaned, 'and now he wants rid of me. The cold, damp sod for me, the warm bosom of Holy Mother Church for him.' She had evidently played this part before.

Jack stepped across to me and exploded in my ear. 'Care

for a nice cup of tea, Father?' My gesture of acceptance could not have been demonstrative enough. 'P'raps another time, then,' he said.

The scene was so dismal, so Dickensian, I couldn't wait to get out. 'You're not in any pain, Mrs Hately?' I said, preparing to leave.

'Never in anything else.' After a gesture of disgust in Jack's direction, she turned her face to the black and peeling wall.

'There, there,' cried Jack. He sat quite still, the tears pouring down his cheeks. 'There, there, me love, me precious.' Her back was iced against him. 'I'm never going to leave you, me dearest, never.'

I moved nearer to his wife to give her my blessing. There was no thawing of the little iceberg in the bed, so I blessed her from behind. With a large, scaly fist, Jack signed himself.

When I left the room that was a house, he was still crying and a deaf old woman was resolutely turned towards the wall.

'Mrs Pring informs me that you went to the Hatelys, Father Neil.' I was at my desk preparing Sunday's sermon. Fr Duddleswell said, 'You were not to know, lad.'

'That they are living in sin?'

He looked startled and wanted to know what I meant. I said I had worked it out that there must have been a previous marriage and divorce, as in the case of Mr Bingley.

'Nothing of the sort,' sighed Fr Duddleswell, sinking into a chair. 'Steel yourself, lad, while I tell you the whole unsavoury tale.' I was in no mood for the facts of life. 'You see,' he said, secretively, 'not to put too fine a point on it, Jack Hately is a priest.'

It was my turn to look startled.

'Now do not take it too hard, Father Neil. These things

happen, if you're still with me.' He outlined the story.

Jack Hately, now eighty-three, left the priesthood in his late thirties and married Betty, 'his partner,' in the Register Office. There had been two children. The first appeared 'far too soon' after they married. Both had emigrated to Australia.

Jack had been faithful to Betty according to his lights. He had worked hard as a postman and was not long retired when a land mine during the war sliced off the top two stories of his house. They had lived in the basement ever since.

Old Jack never went to church. He probably couldn't see the point because he and Betty were excommunicated and he was bitter as well. When an Indian Bishop came to St Jude's to appeal for money, Fr Duddleswell took him to see the Hatelys. He couldn't converse with Jack who was already deafer than a pillar-box, but as he was leaving, the Bishop knelt down. Jack gathered he was asking *him* for his blessing. 'Well, strike a light, Father Neil. Old Jack had not seen the inside of a church for more than forty years and here was a coffee-coloured Bishop kneeling at his feet, begging his blessing.'

Jack started going to Mass again. He couldn't receive Holy Communion, of course. Mrs Hately could because she was in danger of death and Catholics are entitled to lots of things in danger of death. Then eighteen months ago Jack came to the presbytery to say he wanted to apply to Rome to have his excommunication lifted. This explained Mrs Hately's fear that the Church was going to take Jack away from her. She was doubly upset at the moment because Fr Duddleswell had received word from Bishop's House that Rome had at last replied to Jack's appeal.

'Tomorrow,' said Fr Duddleswell, 'I am off to see the Vicar General to hear what Rome has decreed.'

As soon as he returned from Bishop's House next day at 11.30, he called for a cup of coffee, 'the strongest the handle will take, Mrs Pring, if you please.'

After that, he took a large white envelope from his brief-case and drew out of it a Latin document footed by a big red seal. The gist of it was that the excommunication could be lifted provided Jack and Betty swore solemnly to live hence-forward as brother and sister.

Fr Duddleswell slapped the document like a naughty child.

'According to this, Father Neil, should there be one sexual lapse on Jack's part, he will re-incur all past censures and we will have to start the long judicial process all over again.'

'That's inhuman,' I gasped.

'But very wise, very *worldly* wise, would you not say, Father Neil? Mother Church realizes only too well that the flesh is weak.'

I protested. 'Father, Jack's eighty-three. His flesh is far too feeble to be weak.' But I had to admit that at his age and with his wife a permanent invalid, their living together as brother and sister was not too harsh an imposition.

Fr Duddleswell guessed that what would upset Betty Hately most was a condition laid down by the Vicar General. To ensure that Rome's terms were carried out to the letter, he personally decreed that Jack and Betty had to sleep in separate rooms. 'When I told him, Father Neil, that they only have one room, he insisted that at least Jack and Betty should have separate beds.'

'Poor old sods,' I said.

Fr Duddleswell did not reprimand me but he said quietly

and firmly as if to silence insubordination, 'Jack is a priest, you follow, Father Neil? He may die soon and the V.G. wishes him to die in his own bed not in hers.'

I did not accompany Fr Duddleswell when he briefed the Hatelys on Rome's decision. He came back, not too dispirited, to report that the old lady had sung her usual lament and started once more to outstare the wall. She had cheered up, though, when she learned that Jack was not about to leave home, after all.

'Now, Father Neil, there is the little matter of a pair of single beds.'

At Franklin's Store, Fr Duddleswell went into a huddle with the manager of the bedding department. It was a slack period and the manager agreed to two divan beds being delivered immediately.

We were at 3 Springfield Road half an hour later when the van arrived. The delivery men screwed on the legs and, to my surprise, joined the divans together to make one double bed.

Fr Duddleswell winked at me. 'Father Neil,' he joked, 'in me seminary days we used to say: beware of bulls and canon lawyers. They have minds like razors, you see, as sharp and as narrow. Better to let 'em have their own way, don't y'think?'

Jack Hately was delighted to have the best of both worlds: to sleep next to his wife and yet have a bed of his own. He lay down on it, sat on it, and bumped up and down on it.

As we were leaving, Fr Duddleswell slipped Jack a fiver which he pocketed out of sight of his arthritic mate. Then we drove off.

On the homeward journey, I said I thought it would be more merciful of the Church to dispense priests like Jack from the vow of celibacy if they wish to marry.

To my surprise, Fr Duddleswell was vehemently opposed to the idea. 'Merciful?' he exclaimed. 'Merciful? To whom, Father Neil? Tell me that, now. Is not the Church's first concern for the majority of priests who do not give up their Latin to run off with women? And are not those who stay confirmed in their vow by the Church's firmness in never granting dispensations?' He whistled through clenched teeth. 'Priests who are tempted to wed in the Register Office are mightily dissuaded by the knowledge that they will never be able to marry in the sight of God or offer a woman the blessing of a Christian home.'

It seemed to me that Jack must have felt as lonely as a sparrow on a roof top when he teamed up with Betty. 'What about special cases?' I asked.

'Father Neil, believe you me, *all* cases are special. The strength of our Church lies in the fact that her rules are bent for nobody. She will no more allow a divorced barmaid to remarry than King Henry VIII. She will no more dispense a priest one year in the ministry than one who is middle-aged with a dozen illegitimate children to his discredit. Everybody, priest and layman alike, knows exactly where he stands.'

He went on to give me a sharp lesson on the value of celibacy. In the seminary, we had learned that priests do not marry so that, freed from domestic ties, they can look after their people day and night. Fr Duddleswell had an altogether broader vision.

For him, a priest is 'no tin cock on a church steeple'. The whole system of Catholicism, its ethic, its creed and its discipline, rests on priestly celibacy. It is celibacy that gives the priest moral authority to teach unpalatable truths. He may be out of touch in many things but none of his congregation ever doubts that he has freely made an enormous sacrifice

194

for their sake. He has the *right* to hand on the tough Catholic teaching on birth-control, abortion, divorce and homo-sexuality because he is a sign of Jesus lonely and crucified in their midst. 'In the priest, Father Neil, sex bows its lovely head to something lovelier: self-sacrifice.'

I had had recent experience of what he meant.

'Furthermore, Father Neil', he said peering through the windscreen as if he were gazing at some impossibly hideous futuristic vision, 'should the Church ever relax her discipline on celibacy, the whole pack of cards will come tumbling down. Even bishops will be found making exceptions in special cases to birth-control and divorce. The good sisters, seeing the laxity of the clergy, will themselves leave their convents like flocks of migrating birds. And in the end, we will have Catholics advocating euthanasia for babies born handicapped and for old people who are incurably ill or a burden on the community.' He was silent for a few moments before adding, 'Merciful, he says. *Merciful.*'

We had reached the garage gates. I prepared to jump out and open up for him but he touched my arm. 'One more thing to further your education, lad.' I looked at him won-dering what next. 'The Vicar General said that Bishop O'Reilly wants me to persuade Betty to retire to an old folks' home. She will be well looked after there and he will foot all the bills.'

'And old Jack?' I said, shocked at the prospect for one so near the grave.

He leaned his forearms on the wheel. 'The Bishop would like him to go into the Dogs' House.' This was the clergy's name for the Monastery of St Michael's, a kind of reforma-tory for naughty priests. 'The Bishop's idea, Father Neil, is that Jack should end his days there. After a few months, Rome might be prevailed on to let the Prodigal say Mass again. That way, he could die with dignity.'

However impressive the principle of celibacy, this was too much for my stomach. 'Father,' I burst out angrily, 'Mrs Hately's old and infirm and in constant pain. *I* think Jack has a duty to stay with her as long as she lives.'

'Whatever the Bishop says?'

I didn't hesitate. 'Yes, whatever the Bishop says.'

Fr Duddleswell looked at me with wrath all over his face. 'Young man,' he snapped, 'have you no regard for the wishes of your Superior and father in God? Get out with you and open that gate.' I rose but before I could slam the door on him, he leaned over and said, 'I tell you this, Father Neil. If old Jack should ever leave his Missis after all these years, I will knock his bloody block off.'

Ten

THE SEASON OF GOOD WILL

Fr Duddleswell told me at breakfast of his decision to invite the Rev. Percival Probble, the Anglican Vicar, and 'his good lady' to tea.

'He is convinced, you see, that at the summer swimming gala he saved me from a watery grave.' I could not deny it. 'I have no wish to disabuse him and so injure his self-esteem.'

Mrs Pring put the dishes down with a clatter which showed what she thought of serving a clergyman's wife at our table.

Fr Duddleswell was looking for support. 'What do *you* think, lad?' Honesty compelled me to say that Mrs Pring's opinion should be taken into consideration. What I meant was that she was, in a sense, our good lady and she never ate with us.

'Well, then,' said Fr Duddleswell, 'that makes a slender majority of one to two in me favour.' He obviously did not count votes, he weighed them. When Mrs Pring walked off in a huff, he said, 'That will muffle her clapper for a while.'

The prospect of tea with a married cleric reminded him of the time he had been on a pilgrimage to Rome before the war. In his Hotel just off the Veneto was an Anglican bishop who was well and truly *'conjugally' matrimonified.* 'Now, Father Neil, the waiters in the restaurant were so flabbergasted that the Bishop, *il Vescovo*, should have a family that they called his wife *la Vescova* and the kiddies *i Vescovini.*'

He was shaking with mirth.

'Did they?'

My dry response dampened his ebullience. 'I suppose, Father Neil, you would have to know Italian to appreciate the finer points of the joke.' I kept silent to tease him further. 'It seemed strange to them, you follow? that a man in a Roman collar should have a wife and *bambini*.'

'Why strange?'

He said lamely, 'They were not used to it.'

'Is something "strange", Father, simply because an Italian waiter in an Italian restaurant in Italian Italy is not used to it?' He must have thought a little divil had got into me that morning. 'Didn't you tell them, Father, that St Peter who emigrated to Italy had a mother-in-law and so presumably a good lady of his own?'

He was in rapid retreat. 'I did not think of it, like.'

'More's the pity,' I said, sucking in the air like soup. 'Those Italian waiters would have been very droll on the topic, I'm sure. Imagine, now, the first *Papa* having a *Papava* and, who knows, even a few *Papavini*?'

He slid off the end of the conversation by rising to his feet and saying his Grace-after-meals in a single movement. 'I've fixed tay for tomorrow at four. Sharp. And, remember, Father Neil,' he bawled, ' 'tis the season of good will to all.' He slammed the door behind him.

Mrs Probble over tea reinforced every argument I had ever heard in favour of celibacy. Obese and topped by a plumed hat of Royal Ascot dimensions, she was one long verbalized stream of consciousness.

When the Vicar managed to edge in a word and attributed Christ's prayer, 'That they may be one' to Luke instead of John, Mrs Probble squawked at him, 'Husband, I *told* you to leave the theology to me.'

She was intrigued to know how we made so much money each year on our Bazaar. She herself toiled like a Trojan to make a success of St Luke's Garden Fête with the most meagre results. 'How *do* you manage it, Fr Duddleswell?' She pronounced it Duddle-swell.

My parish priest explained to 'Mrs Prob-bull' that we Catholic priests have more numerous female helpers than Solomon himself. Their womanly hearts are so touched by our masculine ineptitude that they rally round us without needing to ask.

Mrs Probble seemed to contemplate for an instant the possibility that she was a liability to her husband and not the huge asset she had always presumed. 'Is that how you explain it?' she said.

'Now, it can hardly be sex-appeal, can it, Mrs Prob-bull?'

'Evidently not,' replied the Vicar's good lady haughtily. If she replied less haughtily than she might have done, it was because she had a favour to ask for her husband. On the last Sunday before Christmas, St Luke's was to have a visitation from the Anglican Bishop of the diocese. A social gathering had been organized to greet him in St Luke's Church Hall. Fr Duddleswell must know that Anglicans, for all their deeply held Christian beliefs, were not so good at attending as Roman Catholics. And what Mrs Probble wanted to ask, as did the Rev. Mr Probble, of course, was this: Would Fr Duddleswell, in the spirit of the season, bring some of his own flock to swell the numbers?

As the request unfolded, I could see Fr Duddleswell's good will being stretched to its limits. He disliked intensely the ascription of episcopacy to a 'doubtfully baptized Anglican layman'. He also loathed the idea of any remotely religious association with those 'Church of England cuckoos who threw us out of our nest.'

The Rev. Mr Probble, sensitive to Fr Duddleswell's religious scruples, assured him that they were cancelling Evensong. It was to be a simple fraternal with beer laid on for those who wanted it. Fr Duddleswell's Benediction of the Blessed Sacrament was at 5.30, which would enable him to bring as many of St Jude's congregation to St Luke's at six o'clock as had a mind to come.

Fr Duddleswell listened in silence as the Vicar explained that to have three Anglican clergy present, and only the usual twenty to thirty of their parishioners, would not create a very fortunate impression on Bishop Pontin—another wince from my parish priest.

It was Mrs Probble who let the cat out of the bag. 'It will so help Percival's preferment, you see, Fr Duddleswell.' She pronounced his name this time with meticulous accuracy.

The Rev. Mr Probble was man enough to admit that he had his eye on a Cathedral canonry, 'but far be it from me, Father, to ask you to violate your Catholic conscience.' It was a good pay-off line.

Fr Duddleswell eyed me to see if I was voting with him but I stayed disenfranchised. 'You promise me, Vicar, no Evensong?'

The Vicar gave his word and made things easier by pointing out that our co-religionist Councillor, Albert Appleby the Mayor, had graciously accepted his invitation to meet the Bishop.

When the Vicar and his wife had left, Fr Duddleswell tried to make light of his defeat. 'I am not one to renege on me debts,' he said, 'when there is no matter of principle involved.' Then changing the subject with a rueful laugh: 'Such is the "felicity of unbounded domesticity".'

His laughter became less forced when I replied, 'The

Vicar, now, he is a regular Duke of Plaza-Toro and no mistake.'

Preparations for Christmas began in earnest. Paper chains and bells were hung in the hall and the dining room. Dangling from the ceiling above Fr Duddleswell's chair, in hope forlorn, was a sprig of mistletoe. The large plaster figures for the crib were taken down from the organ loft and given their annual dusting.

Mrs Pring was stirring silver threepenny pieces into the Christmas cake-mix, as thick as cement, in an enormous bowl. I heard Fr Duddleswell tell her that he would provide the turkey.

The carols on the radio attuned our minds to the peace and good will of the festive season. I had even arranged for Mrs Rollings to be received into the Church on Christmas Eve. She was not ready for it and never would be, but at least, with Christmas over, I could begin the new year without the prospect of instructing her every couple of weeks.

The mood started to change on Fr Duddleswell's last day off before Christmas. In the afternoon, Mrs Pring went to Siddenhall to visit her daughter. Being at a loose end, I donned an old polo-necked pullover and gumboots and pottered around in the garden. The weather had turned mild and I put in a spot of digging with the garden fork. I was well stationed to hear the telephone and the front door bell.

It was the side door bell that rang about 3.15 just as dusk was coming on. Standing there were two sturdy, clean-cut young men in dark suits. At first, I thought they were policemen in plain clothes. One of them put his foot in the door while the other thrust a huge open book in front of my nose. It was too black to see but I smelled it was a Bible. Having only a garden tool in my hand I was at a disadvantage.

'May we come in, Brother?' said Brother Frank, the Bible-bearer, in an American accent, pushing past me. I did not like being addressed below my rank but what could I do?

They carried me with them into Mrs Pring's kitchen and deposited me in a chair at the table. Brother Frank and Brother Hank sat down opposite me and told me that they represented the Church of Christ Shepherd.

Was I a Christian? A Catholic, gee. Well, they wanted to tell me there and then that in their eyes nobody was beyond the mercy of God.

They had a beautiful message for me personally, from Jesus, if only my eyes were not blind and my ears not deaf.

There followed a long but speedy history of 'the fastest growing religious movement in the history of this planet.' I would be relieved to know that their beautiful Founder, the divine Father Shepherd from Scranton, Pennsylvania, had no hang-ups about sex, indeed he positively encouraged the exercise of 'all these beautiful faculties', and they could prove his assertions from this beautiful and holy Book.

Now to the nitty-gritty. In the Church of Christ Shepherd, every member had to freely contribute the biblical tithe of his salary. 'So how much do *you* earn, Brother?' asked Brother Hank, advancing keenly.

I was so surprised at being allowed to speak I couldn't get the words out. After further encouragement, I said, 'Forty pounds a year.'

'Are you on welfare, Brother?' said Brother Frank.

'No, I'm a Roman Catholic priest.'

'Jesus Christ!' they exclaimed in chorus. I instinctively bowed my head, followed them as they raced to the door and bolted it after them. They couldn't have made a quicker exit had I admitted to being a leper.

In the morning, Mrs Pring took me aside. 'Any visitors

yesterday, Father Neil?'

I said that two religious cranks had tried to convert me. 'Why?'

'Because,' she whispered, 'the clock on my mantelpiece went missing.'

I apologized and promised I would buy her another for Christmas. She wouldn't hear of it. It had never worked and was purely ornamental. If she raked around in the garden, she said, she would probably find it there. At least, they hadn't stolen the new Hoover.

I thanked her for not splitting on me to Fr D. In my heart, I could not be sure the young men had taken the clock. I hadn't seen them take it and they seemed sincere. What made me furious was their vicious method of evangelization. They muscled in, took over your castle and brought out the worst in you. I was glad Catholics did not brow-beat people like that.

Later, above the cooing of pigeons, I heard Fr Duddleswell talking to Billy Buzzle the Bookie across the garden fence. 'Seeing 'tis the season of good will,' Father Duddleswell had tossed Pontius, Billy's black Labrador, an enormous bone. Billy was maintaining that two of our flock had knocked on his door the afternoon before and tried to convert him. Fr Duddleswell replied that none of his parishioners was stupid enough to attempt any such impossible thing.

'They had Irish brogues and they wanted to sell me a Bible,' said Billy. This was proof for Fr Duddleswell that they were none of his. Orangemen at worst. Catholics rely on the teaching authority of the Church and do not go in for Bible-hawking.

'Anyway, Fr O'Duddleswell,' said Billy, 'they didn't succeed. I persuaded them instead to put £5 at 10 to 1 on

Twinkletoes in the 3.00 at Plumpton. It came in last.'

He asked Fr Duddleswell if he would care for a little wager himself. It was already snowing in Scotland, Yorkshire and North Wales. Billy would bet £5 even money that it would snow in Fairwater in the next three days. Fr Duddleswell said that, whatever the forecast, his rheumatics told him the opposite. The final terms agreed were these: If it snowed within three days, Fr Duddleswell would fork out £5. If it didn't Billy would give Fr Duddleswell a ten foot Christmas tree for the church, and a fifteen pound turkey.

A large round thrush alighted on the fence in time to see the two men, in the spirit of the season, shake hands on it.

My mood darkened further when Mrs Rollings came for her final instruction prior to her reception. I had run through the ceremony with her including the mechanics of confession when she burst out, 'I don't know how to say this, Father.' She found a way to tell me that, while she accepted without argument the Catholic doctrine on Hell, Indulgences, Papal Infallibility, the Real Presence of Christ in the Blessed Sacrament and the Virgin Birth, she could not agree with the teaching on birth-control.

If she had broken the news to me three months before I would have rejoiced. I had not wanted her in the first place, but to lose her after all that agony was hurtful and humiliating. On reflection, was it naïve of me not to realize that something might be wrong with her marriage when she had twins of eight and no more children?

I had to be true to my convictions. There could be no compromise on a matter of principle and I had no intention of brow-beating her in the manner of those phoney evangelists.

We shook hands on the doorstep and said our last goodbye. I would not have believed it possible but there were tears in her eyes as she left and not a few pangs in my heart, too.

I told Fr Duddleswell the bad news at the first opportunity. He treated it as a huge joke. As far as he was concerned there was no question of me losing my first scalp. He paid tribute to my long-suffering.

I wanted to know how he could take it so lightly.

'Well, you see, Father Neil, in ethical matters I am far more concerned that she practises what the Church preaches than gives it her full-hearted consent. I have already assured the Bishop that she will be a model Catholic, at least in that respect.'

I said it was a mystery to me how he expected Mrs Rollings to practise what she did not believe in.

'To tell the truth,' he said, ' 'twould be needless expense on her part to contravene the Church's law and 'twould require the operation of the Angel Gabriel for her to conceive again.' He explained that 'the necessary equipment' had been taken from her after the twins were born.

He immediately got on the phone to the baker. 'Wilf,' he said, 'get your woman over here on Christmas Eve at 8 a.m. sharp. Fr Boyd will do the drowning himself.'

Fr Duddleswell's rheumatics proved an accurate barometer. A tall Christmas tree was duly delivered to the church and a turkey to the presbytery with a terse note attached to its neck: TO THE LUCK OF THE IRISH. Fr Duddleswell pinched his arm and prophesied that God would not whiten the world before Christmas Day itself.

On the evening of Sunday December 22nd, Fr Duddleswell conducted a short Benediction with the three standard hymns, *O Salutaris*, *Tantum Ergo* and *Adoremus*. The hundred or so present were reinforced by members of the Legion of Mary, the Saint Vincent de Paul Society and the Union of Catholic Mothers, as well as various unattached parishioners who had heard rumours of free Anglican beer.

By 5.45, Fr Duddleswell and I led our well-muffled army through the streets of Fairwater singing carols. A thoughtful Irishman, Paddy Feeney, took a collection from the passers-by on our way. There must have been two-hundred of us.

In ten minutes we were in the warm climate of St Luke's Church Hall. The Anglican clergy and their wives and about twenty parishioners were waiting to greet us. On the stroke of six, the Mayor arrived and, soon, Bishop Pontin, modestly dressed by Catholic standards in a black suit with a clerical collar above a purple stock.

The Rev. Mr Probble introduced Fr Duddleswell and me to the Bishop, adding barely coherent comments on the excellence of inter-Church relationships in Fairwater.

The Bishop, speaking Oxford English, thanked Fr Duddleswell for bringing along one or two of his parishioners.

'Or three or four, sir,' replied Fr Duddleswell.

After thirty minutes of eating and drinking in small groups, the Vicar clapped his hands at a signal from Mrs Probble to announce that the fraternal would have to close until the Carol Concert in the church was over.

Fr Duddleswell, who had no idea it was going to begin, was furious at the deception practised upon him by his opposite number. The Mayor, forewarned no doubt, took him by the shoulder. 'Don't be upset, Farver,' he whispered. 'It's Mrs Probble's doing. No 'arm. I'm attending it myself.'

'Well may you, Bert, but I have no official position to maintain, d'you hear? To enter that mausoleum would be tantamount to *communicatio in sacris*. 'Twould be to desecrate all within me that is holy.' He gritted his teeth. 'I am withdrawing meself, me curate and me entire flock.'

'Farver, Farver,' pleaded Mr Appleby, 'you can't do that in the season of good will.' He argued that if angels could sing hymns for Jewish shepherds, there was nothing to stop Catholics singing a few carols for the conversion of Protestants. 'Besides, Farver,' he said, 'I am officially deputing you to act in this civil function. You can give out the food parcels to the old-age pensioners.' A bus load of them were at that very moment stepping down and trooping into the church.

That seemed to pacify Fr Duddleswell's conscience. Before the Vicar invited him to accompany the Bishop to the vestry, I saw Mayor Appleby slip Fr Duddleswell his own small mother of pearl rosary.

We were into the third carol before Fr Duddleswell appeared. In spite of the disguise, there was no doubting the fact that it *was* indeed he, dressed as Father Christmas. At least he wasn't required to sing with us—and the beard hid his blushes.

He told me afterwards that his being cheated in earnest was all made worthwhile by the Bishop remarking to the Rev. and Mrs Probble in his hearing.

'Percy, my dear fellow, I do congratulate you on having so many devout Irishmen in your congregation.'

Just before 8 o'clock next morning, Mrs Rollings appeared white-faced in the sacristy as I was preparing to vest. She was clutching a Catholic Truth Society pamphlet in which was printed the ceremony for the reception of a convert. She was worried that in the part about abjuring heresies she would have to denounce totally her former religious upbringing and all its errors.

'I can't say it, Father,' she sniffled.

I tried an entirely different approach. 'All right, Mrs Rollings,' I said ironically, 'if you can't say it, try whispering it.'

Instead of slapping my face, she brightened up immediately. 'It won't be so bad like that, will it, Father?' and she returned to the front bench to join her family.

Everything went well until her confession. I led her down the church to the confessional. Before I could stop her she had gone into my side and closed the door. It took some time to sort it out and get her kneeling on the prie-dieu in her proper place. She was muttering something about the 'number and species of all my mortal sins'.

Fr Duddleswell's opinion was that there are basically two types of female penitents. Those that suffer verbally from either diarrhoea or constipation. 'The latter sort,' he had said, 'need a liberal laxative of kindness.'

Mrs Rollings was of the latter sort when it came to confessing her sins and I was running out of kindness. The confession took fully twenty minutes. I did not know if she had got everything off her chest. If it was still a bit grimy, I consoled myself with the thought that it was her responsibility not mine.

When it came to the conditional baptism, I longed for the return of the ancient practice of three-fold total immersion. After all, I had a strong right arm.

Of course, I was sorry for my wicked thoughts afterwards and deeply humbled when I saw the joy on the faces of the Rollings family. The nominal head of it took me aside when Mass was over. 'Fr Boyd, since my wife started her instructions, she is a different person.'

'So am I, Mr Rollings,' I said.

All dismal reflections were banished by the approach of Christmas and the birth of Christ. Ever since I was a child, the highlight for me has been Midnight Mass.

The church looked gorgeous with its flowers and potted plants, the lights and decorations on the Christmas tree and the crib with the Babe in the manger.

Some strong men in the parish had been deputed to bring a couple of hundred extra stacking chairs from Tipton Hall and to keep out the drunks. Fr Duddleswell and I, clad in cassock and biretta, began by greeting the parishioners as they trooped in smilingly.

The Rollings family was there and old Jack Hately and Mrs Dodson and Dr Daley and Lord Mitchin and Mr Appleby with his wife. To my great joy, Archie and Peregrine arrived early and sat in the front row. It hurt me that Fr Duddleswell should tell me to make sure 'that fine pair keep their hands out of the till'.

Mr Bottesford, the undertaker, sneaked in and sat at the back like a publican. Mother Stephen led a representation from the Convent. Even Billy Buzzle put in a brief appearance to cast his eye over his Christmas tree. 'Tell you what, Fr O'Duddleswell,' he said, 'I'd willingly swop my takings for yours tonight.' There was bound to be a congregation of five hundred.

We spent the last quarter of an hour before Mass hearing confessions. When I opened my box to go to the sacristy, who should I see but Nurse Owen with Spinks, the abortionist, in tow? Herod come to worship the Lord, I thought. I could have sworn that his bald patch was now as big as a half crown.

Fr Duddleswell was to sing the Mass and preach while I assisted him. Already the church was bursting at the seams. In the loft, the choir was in full voice. *Adeste fideles* and then *Silent Night, Holy Night*. 'Ah, 'tis enough,' I said, as I helped Fr Duddleswell struggle into his white vestments, 'to turn your taps on.'

His sermon, full of theatrical gestures, was superb. It was received in utter silence. For his text he chose St Paul's words: *Christ, though rich, became poor to enrich us with his poverty.*

He began by calling attention to the Christmas tree, 'donated by a devout parishioner'. That tree was the most Christian of all our symbols. Did not the first Adam eat from a tree in disobedience to God? And did not the second Adam, Jesus, eat the bitter fruit of another tree out of obedience to God His Father? Legend has it that the cross of Calvary was planted in the very spot where once grew the tree of the knowledge of good and evil.

Was not the Christmas tree itself the signal proof of God's power to bring life out of death? Here it was, green wood in the deadness of the year. Like a Child born of a Virgin Mother. Like resurrection following upon Calvary's death when our Lord and Saviour Jesus Christ flew on His wooden bird to God the Father.

God, according to Fr Duddleswell, is deviousness carried to infinity. He quoted Crashaw's lines on the birth of Christ:

> *Welcome all wonders in one sight!*
> *Eternity shut in a span,*
> *Summer in winter, day in night,*
> *Heaven in earth and God in man.*

Jesus forsook his eternity to enter time. He gave up His infinite riches to become poor for us and to enrich us with His poverty. He forsook the bosom of His Father for birth in a cave. None of this could have happened had not God humbled Himself to become as a child in order to enter the Kingdom of Man. God planned it so that Mary the Virgin would be her Maker's maker and her Father's mother.

And what is the meaning of all this?

'That we, me dear people, should ourselves forsake guile to merit the blessing God gives to the weak and foolish of the world. That we should forsake our love of earthly riches for the sake of the spiritual blessings brought to us in abundance by the poor little Babe of Bethlehem.'

Throughout the recitation of the Creed that followed the sermon, the congregation were rustling through pockets and purses to forsake some of their money. The Christmas offering, the most generous of the year, is by tradition the personal gift of Catholics to their priests. As the collection was being harvested, glimpsing out of the corner of my eye, I could only marvel at the sight of the notes mounting in a dozen plates borne by the parish jury of twelve just men. I was already contemplating buying Meg and Jenny a bicycle each.

So eloquent was the sermon, so beautiful the singing, that for the first time I could remember there was no mass exodus of parishioners as soon as the celebrant gave the last blessing.

Fr Duddleswell and I put on our birettas prior to leaving the sanctuary. He handed me the precious tabernacle key saying, 'Put this in the safe, Father Neil, and then join me in the porch.'

Within a minute, I had locked the key away and, having removed my cotta, joined him at the church door to wish the congregation a happy Christmas as they threaded between us.

When we were left alone, Fr Duddleswell locked the front door and we retired to the sacristy where he unvested.

'Ah, Father Neil,' he said, 'the old saying is true: the Christmas midnight Mass equals twenty-one Masses.'

He was the first to notice that there was something disturbing about the collection plates. They contained only silver and the usual assortment of brass with Irish pennies predominating. The notes, the cheques, and the envelopes specially designed to hold the offering of a whole family had disappeared.

My heart experienced a great pang when I saw what the loss of the money meant to him. He seemed so unexpectedly vulnerable.

'There must have been nigh on £300 in notes,' he gulped. 'Have you any idea where the divil it can be, Father Neil?'

Half jokingly I said, 'Search me, Father,' and turned my cassock pockets inside out to reveal nothing but a bunch of keys. As an afterthought, I asked, 'This is serious, isn't it, Father? You're not having me on?'

He did not hear me. He was muttering something about cash being the only thing not covered by the insurance. He opened the door leading to the house and asked Mrs Pring if she had taken the big money into the presbytery for protection. I heard Mrs Pring deny stridently that in all these years she had laid one finger on his filthy lucre.

I helped him search the vestment drawers and cupboards. We looked into the confessionals and he even rummaged in the straw of the crib. Not a smell of it.

'Father Neil,' he sighed in desperation. 'I want you to dial 999 and get the police here immediately.'

When I returned a couple of minutes later, the lights in the church were ablaze. I saw him turf the baby Jesus out of his crib in case the thief had temporarily hidden the loot there.

We unbolted the front door and stood there waiting for the police. 'Did they give you any indication when they would arrive, Father Neil?'

I said no. The police prided themselves on answering any

emergency call in any part of London within three minutes but, of course, this *was* Christmas Eve.

Fr Duddleswell's glasses were steaming and he was thumping his arms diagonally against his shoulders to stop himself from shivering.

Outside the church, the scene was one of perfect peace. In the windows of houses across the road the lights of Christmas trees were winking off and on. Smoke from chimneys was ascending like incense to heaven. In that mild winter, a few rose bushes, caught in the shaft of light from the church, could be seen still bearing flowers.

As we waited, he went crazily through the suspects. Archie and Peregrine he accused first. I defended them stoutly. Peregrine was capable of anything but surely Fr Duddleswell remembered how Archie had made him give the doctor back his wallet.

He turned his ire on Billy Buzzle. In revenge for losing his bet. Billy could have climbed the fence, got in through our back door and slipped into the sacristy after the collection. Even Fr Duddleswell discounted this theory. Billy Buzzle, he admitted, was far too crooked to stoop to straightforward theft.

Bottesford, now, what about Bottesford? He certainly had a score to settle. Another ludicrous suggestion. He was a rich man and found it far less hazardous robbing the dead than the living.

Still no sign of the infernal police. He sent me to look in the confessionals again. I reported that I'd had no luck.

'Father,' I said, 'isn't it more likely that the thief is someone without any criminal record who found all that money lying around too great a temptation?'

'One thing, lad,' he said ... 'Oh, where are these bloody police? When they arrive there will be no Silent bloody

Night, Holy bloody Night around here. And they will probably send that brute who biffed you under the counter.' He
was now able to pick up the thread of the thought. 'One
thing, I promise you, lad. *You* will not go short. I will make
it up to you.'

'Please, Father, no,' I replied staunchly. 'If Jesus became
poor for ...'

He interrupted me. 'You cannot sole your shoes on £40 a
year without your fair share of the Christmas offering, you
follow? Neither can I, come to that. Oh, where in heaven's
bloody name are the police?'

Mrs Pring addressed us over our shoulders. 'Isn't it about
time you two men came in from the cold?'

Fr Duddleswell pulled his biretta more firmly down on his
head. 'This is man's work, woman, and we are awaiting the
police.'

Mrs Pring said, 'They're not coming.'

'They are delayed, woman, but they will be here any hour
now.' Mrs Pring was adamant that they were not coming. He
turned to me. 'Father Neil, did you not phone them?'

I carefully removed my biretta and smartly turned it up-
side down so as not to lose any of the precious collection of
notes, cheques and envelopes.

He sat down on the cold step, rubbed his eyes inside his
glasses, puffed, and rubbed his eyes again. Then he sprang
up as if to box my ears.

I took one step backwards. 'Now, remember, Father
Charles, 'tis the season of good will.'

Mrs Pring roared with laughter. He silenced her by giving
her a mistletoe peck on the forehead and wishing her a
merry Christmas.

'Lock up, Fathers,' she said in a snuffly voice. 'I've boiled the kettle and there's an Abishag waiting for each of you in your beds.'

We stayed there together for a few moments longer looking out on to the quiet scene. In the light of the street lamps, we saw the first snow of the winter fall. A large flake settled on my eyelash till I blinked it away.

'Ah, Father Neil,' said Fr Duddleswell serenely, 'are they not the only pure white doves this sordid city sees?' I nodded, half asleep now. Suddenly he turned on me. 'I have something else I have been meaning to say to you.' I didn't think he would let me off that lightly.

He stretched up his arms and embraced me. 'Merry Christmas to you, Neil.'

'Merry Christmas, Father,' I said.